School Secret

Janet Perkins is at th[...]
of junior school life have proved all too much for her.
After all there is more to being a school secretary than
most people imagine. But the answer is near at hand
when Mr Mackintosh, the Head, spots an advertisement for a School Secretary Commando Camp which
revitalizes tired school secretaries.

However, Hairy Harry the Hatchet Man also sees the
ad and with his gang of nasty crooks and the revolting
Mrs Gunge, he hatches a plan to sneak into the camp,
capture the secretaries and hold them to ransom. And
what better time to begin the attack than when the
women are about to embark on a military manoeuvre.
Mrs Perkins has to exercise all her powers of escape,
act quickly under pressure, even complete an assault
course! But can our gallant heroine single-handedly
dodge the villains, save her comrades and win the
battle? Honestly, the things a school secretary has to
do!

Brough Girling was born in 1946, and now lives in
London with his wife and a mad cat. As well as writing
books he has been head of the Children's Book Foun-
dation, and was the first editor of Young Telegraph.
He is founder and director of Readathon, the national
sponsored read that raises money for charity.

By the same author

THE BANGERS AND CHIPS EXPLOSION
DUMBELLINA
THE GREAT PUFFIN JOKE DIRECTORY
THE GREEN AND SCALY BOOK
VERA PRATT AND THE BISHOP'S FALSE
TEETH
VERA PRATT AND THE BALD HEAD
VERA PRATT AND THE FALSE
MOUSTACHES

BROUGH GIRLING

School Secretary
on the Warpath

Illustrated by Tony Blundell

PUFFIN BOOKS

PUFFIN BOOKS

Published by the Penguin Group
Penguin Books Ltd, 27 Wrights Lane, London W8 5TZ, England
Penguin Books USA Inc., 375 Hudson Street, New York, New York 10014, USA
Penguin Books Australia Ltd, Ringwood, Victoria, Australia
Penguin Books Canada Ltd, 10 Alcorn Avenue, Toronto, Ontario, Canada M4V 3B2
Penguin Books (NZ) Ltd, 182–190 Wairau Road, Auckland 10, New Zealand
Penguin Books Ltd, Registered Offices: Harmondsworth, Middlesex, England

Published in Puffin Books 1993
1 3 5 7 9 10 8 6 4 2

Text copyright © Brough Girling, 1993
Illustrations copyright © Tony Blundell, 1993
All rights reserved

The moral right of the author has been asserted

Typeset by Datix International Limited, Bungay, Suffolk
Filmset in 12/14 pt Monophoto Century Schoolbook
Printed in England by Clays Ltd, St Ives plc

Except in the United States of America,
this book is sold subject to the condition
that it shall not, by way of trade or otherwise,
be lent, re-sold, hired out, or otherwise circulated
without the publisher's prior consent in any form of
binding or cover other than that in which it is
published and without a similar condition
including this condition being imposed
on the subsequent purchaser

Author's Note

Readers will notice that all the school secretaries in this book are women. This is not deliberate stereotyping on my part: despite my best endeavours, I have not been able to locate one single solitary male secretary in any of our state junior schools.

The book therefore reflects what is, rather than what should be. I hope readers will allow me this single element of realism. (Oh, and most of the villains are men – that's realistic too!)

Chapter One

*In which we discover a Head
Teacher with a problem*

*

There was a knock on the Head teacher's office door. 'Come in,' said Mr Mackintosh.

If you're a Head Teacher you're never quite sure who is going to interrupt you next, or what it will be about. It's all part of the excitement of the job.

The door opened and Mrs Janet Perkins, the school secretary, stepped into the room.

I don't know if you've read about Mrs Perkins before. In case you haven't I should point out that she is a rather remarkable woman. Although on the outside she looks much like any other school secretary – a kind smile, the occasional frown, and sensible shoes – inside she's as tough as a rhino's big toe. She's got nerves of steel and an outstanding ability to get things fixed, a bit like Superman but without the silly red cloak. (No school sec. would be seen dead in a red cloak!)

Mrs Perkins once rescued the whole of St Gertrude's Junior School, single-handed, following a criminal incident when the school dinners exploded, but that's another story . . .

Mr Mackintosh was pleased to see her. Like every Head Teacher he relies on his school secretary to keep the place running smoothly. She is more valuable to him than all the tea in the staff-room.

'Ah, good morning, Mrs Perkins,' he said, brightly.

'Good morning, Mr Mackintosh,' she replied, but the moment she did so the Head could tell that she was not her normal smiling self. Her voice sounded tense and strained.

'Is something the matter?' he enquired.

'I'm sorry,' said Mrs Perkins, her voice cracking with emotion, 'but there is. I'm at the end of my tether. I just can't cope any longer.'

'Now whatever do you mean?' said Mr Mackintosh, turning pale. The last thing on earth a Head Teacher needs is a school secretary who feels she can't cope.

'This school has finally got me down,' said Mrs Perkins, sinking into the chair opposite his desk. 'All the playground fights, the punching and kicking, the spitting, the swearing – and that's just the teachers.'

Mr Mackintosh went even paler.

She continued: 'The children are just as bad; already this morning I've been down to the Infants to put out a fire, replace a washbasin, and untie poor Mr Jenkins the Games Teacher.'

'Come now, I'm sure it can't be as bad as all that,' said Mr Mackintosh weakly.

'Well, it *is*, Head Teacher! There's much more to being a school secretary than most people imagine; all those forms to fill in, silly parents to deal with, sick to clear up, knees to plaster, lavatories to unblock. Oh, the

9

children are all right most of the time, but people like the kitchen staff are worse than useless, always stealing the food and chewing tobacco. Mrs Gunge, for instance, is a total disgrace.'

Mrs Gunge is Chief Cook and Dinner Lady at St Gertrude's.

Mrs Perkins pulled a handkerchief the size of a scout tent from the sleeve of her treasured green cardigan, and dabbed her nose with it. For a terrible moment Mr Mackintosh thought that she was going to cry.

'I just don't think I can take any more,' said Mrs Perkins. She said it quietly, and he knew that she meant it.

He also knew that he was in trouble. Trying to run a school without a school secretary is like trying to eat a Chinese meal with only one chopstick.

'Oh dear,' he said. 'This is not like you, Mrs Perkins. I really think you need a bit of a rest. I think you should take the day off. Go home and put your feet up. Perhaps you'll feel better in the morning.'

'Well, yes, thank you, Mr Mackintosh, I think I'd better go home. I'm not much use in this state. But are you sure you can manage without me today? There's all the dinner money to collect, and a bus to order for the first year swimmers.'

'Yes, yes – you leave all that to me,' said Mr Mackintosh, a kind smile hiding his sense of utter panic.

Janet Perkins left the room and, as directed, went home.

Mr Mackintosh got up from behind his desk. With a huge sigh he walked over to the window. Outside it was breaktime and he could see Jenny Ferguson and two other girls from the Reception Class pulling up the school tulips and eating them, but he hardly even noticed. He was much too worried about what Mrs Perkins had said to care.

'Oh well,' he said eventually. 'I suppose life must go on. I'd better see about that bus for the first year swimmers.'

He opened a copy of *The Battleground*. It's the Head Teachers' newspaper that tells them how to do their job. He was hoping to look up the phone number of the bus company that the school normally used. Instead he saw something much more important. It was an advertisement which caused his eyes to widen and his jaw to drop open.

I'll tell you a bit later what it said.

Chapter Two

*In which we unfortunately have
to meet Hairy Harry
the Hatchet Man*

*

Later that day, in fact at the very same time
as Mrs J Perkins was at home slipping off
her sensible shoes and putting her sensible
feet up on her sensible footstool, Mr Hairy
Harry the Hatchet Man was relaxing in
another part of town – with a pint of his
special lager-free alcohol.

Hairy Harry the Hatchet Man is one of the
most fearfully frightful villains you could
ever wish not to meet. For a start he's quite
horribly hairy. He's got thick black hair all
over, including the palms of his hands and
between his huge toes. He's like a bear, only
not so well behaved. No bear, for instance,
carries an axe under its overcoat, or picks its
nose with a flick-knife.

I said that Harry was relaxing, but in truth
he was rather bored. He was sitting in his
dingy room in the cellar of a disused building on some wasteland. It was a scene of
utter devastation – far worse than your bed-
room. The floor was covered with old bottles,

cigarette ends, nail parings, apple cores, bones and banana skins. If your mother had seen Hairy Harry's room she would have had a purple fit!

Harry sat on his old broken sofa, put his feet on an upturned beer crate that served as a coffee table, and twiddled his great big hairy thumbs. 'I don't know ...' he mumbled to himself. 'If only there was something **interesting** to do. This is worse than being in prison!' (Hairy Harry knew quite a lot about being in prison.)

He threw his empty beer glass at a passing rat. 'If only some of the lads were "out and about".'

By 'the lads', Harry was almost certainly referring to several of his friends who, when not in prison themselves, had worked with him on various business ventures. These included robberies, ambushes, mass kidnaps, and blackmail, and they'd almost always been accompanied by threatening behaviour, breaches of the peace, and lots of malice aforethought.

I think the individuals Harry had in mind would almost certainly have included Hans Zupp the Hold Up Man, Nigel the Nicker, and Cracker Crawford, explosives expert.

Harry got up from the sofa and kicked an overflowing ashtray across the floor. 'I'm so

bloomin' bored!' he said out loud.

He glanced down idly at the page of an old copy of *The Battleground* that had once contained his fish and chips, but was now lying near a puddle at his feet.

An advertisement caught his eye, and almost as soon as it did so it set Harry's small, slow, criminal mind in action.

As a matter of fact, it was the same advert that Mr Mackintosh had seen in the last chapter – the one that caused his eyes to widen and his jaw to drop.

This is what it said:

HEAD TEACHERS!

HAS YOUR SCHOOL SECRETARY'S 'GET UP AND GO' GOT UP AND GONE?

Is she finding it difficult to cope?
Tired? Listless? Not as fast as she was
over 1,000 metres?

SEND HER TO US!

THE SCHOOL SECRETARY COMMANDO CAMP!

REVITALIZING TIRED SCHOOL SECRETARIES OUR SPECIALITY!

*We make the SAS look like
a pack of Brownies!*

TRAINING COURSES INCLUDE:

Fitness & Body-
building

Initiative testing

Map reading

Adventure training

Unarmed Combat

Guerrilla Warfare

Riot Control –
Advanced and Basic Techniques

Our Motto: *She who Cares, Wins!*

Chapter Three

*Another problem for
the Head Teacher!*

*

When Mr Mackintosh arrived at St Gertrude's the next morning he was pleased to see Mrs Perkins standing in the foyer on the lookout for latecomers.

'Good morning, Mrs Perkins,' he said, 'I hope you're feeling a bit better this morning.'

'Well, a little, thank you, Head Teacher,' she replied, but her voice still didn't have the usual spring in its step.

'Come in and see me when classes have started; I've come across something that may be just what you need.'

'Very well, Mr Mackintosh,' she said. Then she went down the corridor to attend to a fallen infant.

Mr Mackintosh went into his office to get his books for Assembly.

Bells rang, announcements were announced, hymns were sung (not very well) and slowly St Gertrude's settled itself into another busy school day.

*

By about ten o'clock – when registers had been taken to classrooms and Billy Baxter, Brian Fottleton, Gopal Bannergee, Sharon White, Belinda Bollard, all the rest of 4B and the children in the other classes admitted that they were present (at least in body, even if their minds were somewhere else) and various bits of money had been collected for dinners, swimming, bookshop etc. – Janet Perkins was happy that everything was in sufficiently good order to allow her to keep her appointment with the Head Teacher.

'Come along in, Mrs Perkins,' he said cheerily, in response to her knock. 'Now, I've seen an advert in *The Battleground* that I think is rather interesting.'

'Oh,' said Janet, slightly surprised.

'Yes. It's a special commando training camp where school secretaries who are feeling a bit under the weather, and are finding it difficult to cope, can go to be retrained. Apparently they come back totally refreshed and revitalized, and ready for anything primary school life can throw at them. What do you think?'

'Well, I must say it sounds very interesting.'

'Good, I thought you'd take a positive attitude towards it,' said the Head, pleased with her response. 'As a matter of fact I phoned

the camp yesterday afternoon to find out more. It seems that what they offer can make you feel like a new person! I took the liberty of telling them how you felt yesterday, and they said it's all too common these days for school secs to get laid low by the pressures of modern school life.

'Anyway, today is Friday and they've got a week's course starting on Monday. I think you should go on it. If it's all right with you I'll phone the commando camp and confirm your enrolment.'

'Thank you, Mr Mackintosh,' she replied with a smile. 'I'm sure it's just what I need –

only this morning coming up the drive a couple of boys gave me the slip near the climbing-frame; in the old days I'd have caught them in a couple of strides. I think a bit of revitalization would do me a power of good.'

He smiled, so pleased that a solution to his terrible problem seemed near at hand.

She smiled back: 'I'm very grateful, Head Teacher: I can't live with myself if I'm not doing my job properly, and to the very best of my ability.'

She went back to her office. She sat down at her neat little desk. 'Now then,' she said to herself. 'If I'm going to be away from school all next week, I'll have to make sure I leave everything in really ship-shape order.'

It was typical of Mrs Perkins to think like this. Like all school secretaries she really cares about her school and the pupils in it. 'I think it's my duty . . .' she said, this time out loud, 'to go and have a stern word with Mrs Gunge in the kitchen. So many children have been complaining recently about the food that I fear it could lead to a riot, and Mr Mackintosh would never be able to deal with a riot without me. It might lead to trouble with parents too: that's the last thing he'd need. I'll go and try to talk some sense into her.'

If you have ever been in a junior school –

and I expect you have – you'll already know the amazing but true fact that dinner ladies are either very nice, or very nasty. They're never a bit of both. Nobody knows why this is.

The nice ones are really nice. They dish out chips, stew and soup with a merry smile on their faces and a song in their hearts. They like children, they like food, and they like bringing the two together.

The nasty ones are a different matter altogether, and Mrs Gunge, Chief Cook and Dinner Lady at St Gertrude's is one of the *very* nasty ones.

For a start they look revolting, and Mrs Gunge certainly does. Her skin is damp and greasy and her hair looks like string that a dog's been chewing. On her chin there's a horrible lump with awful white whiskers growing out of it.

Her large forearms look as if they've been badly carved from old Stilton cheese. Her legs are like knobbly cabbage stalks, and there's often half a cigarette dangling from her flabby grey lips. Yuk!

Mrs Perkins has had trouble with Mrs Gunge before – you may have read about it.

When Mrs Perkins arrived in the school kitchen, Mrs Gunge was cutting up raw meat. Her hands, the colour and texture of corned beef, wielded a great kitchen knife with a flourish that Hairy Harry the Hatchet Man would have admired.

'Well, what is it, Mrs Bossy Bum?' asked Mrs Gunge with a snarl.

'I'm going away next week, Mrs Gunge,' said Janet Perkins coolly, 'and I thought I ought to tell you that several children have been to see me recently to complain about your cooking.'

'Oh they have, have they? Bloomin' kids! If I had my way they'd be put down at birth! They ruin this school, they do.'

'They say they don't like the way you make gravy. It's either as thin as old dishwater, or it's so thick they have to carve it with a knife. And they don't like custard with such large lumps in. Last week Susan Davies found a cigarette end in her soup, and Yashpal Singh had a piece of something in his chicken curry that looked to me very much like an old piece of Elastoplast.'

'Well, bad luck!' grunted Mrs Gunge. She brought her knife down on an unsuspecting bit of stewing steak with such force that the kitchen shook.

'I'm not making a formal complaint,' went on Mrs Perkins, 'but with me away and Mr Mackintosh on his own in the office, I hope you'll pull your weight and try to please the children a little more. The Head won't want

parents coming up to school to complain about your food.'

Mrs Gunge grunted.

Mrs Perkins left the kitchen and went back to her office. She spent the rest of the day filling in forms, answering the telephone, writing letters and putting stamps on them. Then she gave her tidy little desk a final tidy, and watered the plant in the pot on her filing cabinet. She fed the school goldfish, said goodbye to Mr Mackintosh and, with his permission, went home to begin her packing ready for her week away at the School Secretary Commando Camp.

Usually Mrs Gunge would have left school long before Mrs Perkins. But today was different. Following the school secretary's visit to the kitchen, Mrs Gunge had been brooding – and there are few things worse than a nasty dinner lady who is brooding.

'*I'll show this flippin' school what's what!*' she said out loud. 'Stupid Mackintosh with his jumped-up secretary and loony teachers and ghastly little kids ... Perkins reckons he'll have a job to run the school without her. Well what if he had to run it without *me*, too?! The brats may moan about my cooking, but they'll moan a whole lot more about none of it! Let's see how old Mackintosh is at making gravy and custard, and stew without fag ends in! I'll go somewhere else and get a new job; that'll show 'em.'

She stormed up to the Head's office. She didn't bother to knock: 'Mackintosh!' she said loudly (he looked up from his desk in amazement) 'I've had enough of this stinking rotten school with its snooty staff and snotty little kids! From now on you can do the blinkin' cooking yerself!'

She didn't bother to look behind her as she stomped out of the room on her revolting, cabbage stalk legs.

If she had she would have seen Mr Mackintosh sitting white-faced at his desk with his head in his hands.

'Next week with no school secretary – and now no cook!'

Chapter Four

*In which Hairy Harry takes
an interesting little walk*

*

When Hairy Harry had first seen the advert about the school secretaries' commando camp, he hadn't really been sure why it was so appealing. He just sensed that somehow a collection of school secretaries, all in one place, should give an inventive and criminal mind something to work on.

Harry doesn't like school secretaries: they are basically kind, caring people, and Harry objects to this. He's never forgotten how the secretary at St Gertrude's got the better of him once. Maybe somehow this training camp would provide a chance for revenge!

As you will have guessed, Hairy Harry the Hatchet Man is quite a slow thinker. He decided that he needed time and space for his mind to work in and that the best way to do this would be to go for a walk.

It was already nearly dark, and there are few things Harry likes better than a stroll down dark alleys, his coat wrapped round his huge, hunched shoulders, and his axe tucked into his broad leather belt.

Outside the air was damp with evening drizzle. Dank swirls of mist hung around the gutters. 'What a delightful evening,' said Harry to himself as he locked his front door and hoofed a couple of milk bottles down the road.

Then, as he reached the end of a particularly dingy little lane, he sensed the presence of another human being.

Harry is by nature a suspicious sort of person – someone who has spent as much time as he has running away from the police, probation officers, prison warders and other criminals, often is.

And now Harry was certain that there was a person standing in a dark doorway about thirty metres ahead of him, on the right.

He slowed his pace and slid his hand inside his coat, just in case. He found the sharpness of his hatchet blade very reassuring, as he tested it with his large hairy misshapen thumb.

If you're as horrible as Hairy Harry (difficult) you're always on the lookout for criminal opportunities. If there *was* a figure in the doorway it might be a fat businessman sheltering from the rain, with a briefcase full of credit cards ... it might be a silly little shopkeeper with a bag full of the day's takings, or wages for his honest little workforce. It might even be a frail little senior citizen on the way back from the Post Office, with a purse full of pension. You never know, it's always best to be ready to do a bit of business.

As Harry got to the doorway he drew his axe and raised it menacingly, shoulder high. He walked forward on tiptoe, stealthily, like a leopard stalking its prey.

He was, therefore, more than a little surprised when the figure, obviously having spotted his approach, stepped from the darkness and spoke to him: 'Well I never! Good evening, Harold!'

'Eh . . . What?'

'I said "Good evening, Harold". It's very nice to see you out and about in the fresh air once more.'

Hairy Harry recognized the owner of the voice and was amazed. It was Police Chief Inspector Bollard. (In case you don't know, his daughter, Belinda, goes to St Gertrude's.)

'Now, look!' said Harry menacingly, but lowering his axe, 'You can't get me for anything this time. I haven't done anything!'

'I never said you had, Harold,' said the Chief Inspector with a rather sarcastic laugh.

'Well I haven't.'

'I know that, sir,' said Chief Inspector Bollard. 'By the way, I've just seen a few of your old friends going into the Slug and Lettuce in the High Street. Quite a lot of your little pals in fact!'

'What do you mean?' said Harry suspiciously.

'Well now,' replied the police officer thoughtfully, 'Hans Zupp was there, and Nigel the Nicker, and Cracker Crawford the safe blower. I hope you won't be joining them, Harold. Me and my men would get *most* interested if you little lot started putting your horrible heads together. I think you know what I mean.'

'Oh no, Chief, I wouldn't even think about it. I was just out for an innocent little walk!'

'Very well, sir,' replied the Chief Inspector, 'I'll wish you good night. Be good, if that's possible in your case!'

Chief Inspector Bollard touched the peak of his flat policeman's hat in a little salute, and strolled off up the road towards a cup of tea in the police station.

Hairy Harry the Hatchet Man stood in the dark doorway until the officer was out of sight, and then he ran as fast as his great hairy legs could carry him, towards the High Street and the Slug and Lettuce . . .!

Chapter Five

A jolly little reunion

*

Sure enough, when Harry slid in through the side door of the Slug and Lettuce in the High Street, there, huddled round a grubby little table, were three of his very best friends.

They were glad to see him, and there was lots of back slapping, and beer buying, and general jollity concerning their reunion.

You may not have met Hairy Harry's partners in crime before, so I'd better introduce them (I warn you now: they're not like the characters you'd read about in a book by Beatrix Potter).

Hans Zupp is short, fat and basically a bank robber. Sometimes he makes do with building societies or even post offices. He's a direct sort of fellow who likes a simple life. He likes to point large revolvers at innocent people and say things like: 'Hand over the cash or I'll blow your block off.' He's not very good at making polite conversation.

Cracker Crawford goes about his work in a much more scientific and subtle way. He's an absolute master at blowing open safes (they are not at all safe if he's around). There's nothing he likes better than lighting blue touch papers, or plunging plungers, or setting really complex timers – anything so long as it's followed by a sky-high explosion. Cracker is the sort of person who makes things go with a bang!

The third of Harry's little party is Nigel the Nicker. He is no less revolting. He steals things – he'd steal the milk out of your tea if you weren't careful. He likes stealing out on a dark night, stealing things, and stealing back home again! Yuk!

When they had swapped all their latest news, and chatted about what the weather had been like recently in places like Dartmoor, Wandsworth and Pentonville, a hush fell over the group, and Harry took the opportunity of making this small speech: 'Lads,' he said. 'I'm specially pleased to see you all here because only today I got the feeling that an opportunity may be about to present itself to us!' This was quite a long sentence for Harry to manage and there was a pause while he drew breath and gave his brain a rest. 'It looks as if, on Monday, a whole group of school secretaries will be gathered together in one place. I feel somehow that should give us the chance to make some big money.'

'What do you mean?' asked Hans.

Cracker Crawford also looked rather puzzled.

But the Nicker was more positive: 'I think you may be right, Harry,' he said, his eyes widening in excitement. 'I've been thinking recently that where we went wrong last time was that we only attacked one school – we weren't thinking BIG enough!'

'We took on a whole school, the teachers

and the secretary!' said Hans, rather indignantly.

'Exactly!' said Nicker. '*One measly school!* We only tried to kidnap the kids from *one* school, and on top of that we didn't take out the school sec. What happened was obvious – she went and rescued them!'

'That's it!' said Hairy Harry. 'We didn't think big enough, did we? We were just messing about! If you want to attack something you aim at the top. To make money out of schools you don't go capturing the kids like we did last time. Kids don't run schools, they're just a nuisance – they're not worth anything. No, we should have realized that if you want to raise money from schools you kidnap and ransom *the school secretary*! That's where the cash is!'

'That's right,' chipped in Cracker Crawford, cottoning on to his leader's thinking. 'Imagine a school without a secretary! It would grind to a halt in about ten minutes! If we could capture a school sec., and then demand money for her safe return, the Head Teacher would work really hard to appeal for funds from the staff and parents. We'd be rolling in loot!'

'It'd be like capturing the most precious prince from the world's wealthiest royal family,' added Hans.

'Exactly!' said Harry, a beaming smile lighting up his hairy face. 'But as I'm trying to tell you, *I'm not talking about* **one** *school secretary*! Like I said, there's going to be a whole clutch of them, a gaggle, a pride – or whatever the name for a number of school secs is, at this Commando Training Camp, from next Monday. Just think of that! We capture as many of them as we can get hold of, and we ransom them for cash. There'll be so much chaos the Minister of Education himself will probably pay up. They'll be worth millions!'

'Our only problem,' said Cracker Crawford thoughtfully, rubbing his chin with the palm of his hand, 'will be how to do it. The camp is a military establishment and will be crawling with soldiers. There'll be masses of barbed wire and sentries. It would be impossible unless we could find someone on the inside who could penetrate the defences, and then let us in.'

The gang were thinking about this little problem, rather glumly, when the side door of the pub opened and in walked Mrs Gunge.

'Evening all,' she said, nodding in their direction and looking even more grumpy than usual. 'What are you lot doing out of prison?'

'We've all been released,' said Hairy Harry. 'We're unemployed at the moment, but we're working on a plan to put that right.'

'Oh yea,' said Mrs Gunge. 'I'm out of work too. I've chucked in cooking at that stupid school. Schools would be all right if they didn't have kids and teachers in them. I couldn't stand it any longer, especially what with that Bossy Bum, Mrs Perkins, the school secretary. She got right up my nose.'

'So what are you going to do?' asked Harry, who remembered Mrs Gunge fondly from the time she'd helped him in the siege of St Gertrude's.

'Well, I'm looking for a cooking job in a nice big institution, where they're not too fussy about food. I'd like to get one up on Mrs blinking Perkins too!'

'Let me buy you a drink,' said Harry slowly.

He bought her a drink, and then he and Hans Zupp and Cracker Crawford and the Nicker and Mrs Gunge huddled round a table and began discussing a plan of action in such low voices that no one else could hear what they were saying . . .

Chapter Six

*In which Mrs Perkins
reports for duty*

*

I don't know if you've ever spent a week at a
commando training camp, but I know that
Mrs Perkins hadn't, and that when she got to
the gates that Monday morning she was feeling rather nervous.

When you're nervous the best thing to do
is to pretend not to be, she knew that, so she
walked straight up to Private Peacock, who
was the sentry standing at ease in front of a
small guardhouse, next to the end of a red-
and-white barrier pole. He had a metal helmet
on his head and a short, semi-automatic rifle
was slung from a strap on his shoulder.

'Good morning,' she said. 'My name is Mrs
Perkins and I've come to enrol on the School
Secretaries' Commando Training Course.'

'Very good, madam,' said Private Peacock
crisply and he walked into the guardhouse
and returned with a clipboard. He scanned
down a list of names until he got to the letter
P, ticked off Perkins and said: 'Now then,
madam, if you would proceed down the drive,

past the large assault course in the woods on your right and the rifle range on your left, you'll see a white hut with a notice-board outside it. They'll enrol you there and show you to your quarters.'

'Thank you very much,' said Janet and picking up her small, tidily packed suitcase, she went off up the drive as directed.

She'd never been in a military establishment before and there were many things she liked about the look of it. There were several long low huts set among neat clumps of trees. The drive itself was lined with stones about the size of footballs, painted brilliant white. Everywhere looked very spick and span, almost as if it had been recently dusted and vacuumed.

She found the hut with the notice-board outside it and reported for duty.

'Good morning,' she said to a soldier who was sitting behind a table with more lists of names on it. She noticed he had stripes on the arm of his uniform. 'I'm Mrs Janet Perkins, I've come to join the School Secretaries' Commando Training Course.'

'NAME OF SCHOOL!' said the soldier in such a loud voice that it made Janet jump.

'Oh, St Gertrude's Junior.'

'RIGHT!! Get fell in on the parade ground over there!' and he pointed to some open ground near the far end of the hut. Janet picked up her small suitcase and walked towards it. 'What a rough man,' she thought to herself. 'If one of the children at school was that rude they'd have to stay in over break . . .'

Round the end of the hut Janet Perkins found a huddle of assorted women, standing beside suitcases, all looking rather worried.

She'd only had time to smile and say hallo to a couple of them when the soldier with the stripes on his uniform came striding towards them.

'RIGHT!' he said loudly. 'Stand in three lines, come on! Come on!'

The secretaries eventually got themselves into three sort of lines. The soldier faced them and spoke. Actually he shouted: 'RIGHT, YOU 'ORRIBLE LOT!'

Several of the school secretaries went slightly pale, and a few clenched their fists. 'You are here to be toughened up and revitalized. And it'll be me what does most of the toughening up and revitalization! My name is Corporal Hodgkins, but most of the ladies 'oo have been on one of these wonderful school secretary courses usually ends up callin' me CORPORAL PUNISHMENT! Little joke! GOT IT?'

Most of the secretaries nodded to indicate

that they had indeed got the Corporal's little joke.

'Now, before we send you off to your dormitory to unpack your kit, the Commanding Officer wants a word with you! STAND TO ATTENTION FOR YOUR COMMANDING OFFICER!'

The school secretaries stood to attention, as best they could, as a big khaki-coloured car pulled up beside the parade ground. Janet noticed that it had a little flag in a tiny chrome flagpole fluttering on its bonnet. The driver, a soldier called Bob Wagstaff, leapt out and opened the back door, saluting as he did so.

Corporal Hodgkins also saluted and one or two of the ladies tried to.

A large rotund man emerged from the rear of the car. He had a very red face, a white moustache, and was wearing an immaculate uniform, with lots of badges, pips and medals all over it.

He walked up to the Corporal and said: 'Thank you, Hodgkins.' Then he turned to the new recruits: 'Good morning, ladies!' he smiled.

'That's more like it,' thought Janet. 'A gentleman at last!'

'It's very nice to see you all here. My name is Brigadier Bletherington-Gore and I'm in charge of your training course. I'm sure you're all going to have a simply rippingly good time and that you'll leave here at the end of the week feeling absolutely tip-top, and ready for anything that school life can jolly well chuck at you! We'll make men . . . I mean women . . . of you here, won't we, Corporal?!'

'YES, SIR!' shouted Corporal Hodgkins,

so loudly that the Brigadier ducked slightly, as if a low-flying aircraft had suddenly gone overhead without warning.

'Jolly good, well, I suggest that you all shuffle orf and find your dormitory and what-not, and meet back here later in the morning to collect your boots and uniforms. I've just got to pop and see someone, but I'll be back in about an hour, and then as we say in the army, "let battle commence"! I believe that Corporal Hodgkins here will be starting you orf this afternoon with a little weight-lifting and general body-building – correct, Corporal?'

'Correct, sir!' shouted Corporal Hodgkins, with a force that nearly took the Brigadier's flat hat off.

'Right, I'll leave you all to it,' said the Brigadier and with a wave of his hand and a large beaming smile he got into the back of his official car and was off. Or should I say orf?

Not long after this, while Janet Perkins and the rest of the recruits were being shown to their large dormitory barrack-room, with its hard metal beds, were unpacking their suit-cases into its hard metal lockers, and trying out its few, hard metal chairs, Brigadier Bletherington-Gore was sitting in his office waiting to see the person he'd said he was going to see.

There was a knock at the door. 'Jolly well come in!' said the Brigadier. And in shuffled the person in question.

'Aah, now then, you'd like to be our new cook, is that right?'

'Yea, that's right,' said the person.

'And have you been a cook before?'

'Oh yea, I've been a cook before all right.'

'Good!' said the Brigadier brightly. 'When can you start?'

'Right now,' said the person.

'Jolly good,' said the Brigadier. 'I suggest you go orf to the kitchen and make a start!'

'Yea, I will,' said the person, and she shuffled out of the room on her cabbage stalk legs.

I think you'll have guessed who she was.

Chapter Seven

*In which we learn about
commando camp breakfasts, and
attend a military briefing*

*

At dawn the next morning a trumpet
sounded. It was time to get up at the School
Secretary's Commando Training Camp.

Janet Perkins swung her legs over the edge
of her hard metal bed and put her feet on the
cold floor. She felt a bit stiff and sore after
the body-building exercises that Corporal
Hodgkins had put them through the afternoon before.

'Right, you 'orrible lot!' said Corporal Hodgkins when the school secs had all cleaned
their teeth, made their narrow little beds, and
lined up on the lawn outside their hut. 'I
expects you're all ready for a spot of breakfast!'

'Oh yes, please, Corporal, we certainly are,'
said several of them together. Janet smiled.
She was feeling pretty peckish herself, and
was looking forward to a couple of slices of
thin brown toast with marmalade and a nice
cup of tea.

'Well you can forget it!' said the Corporal with a terrible grin. 'Before you tucks into anything at this camp in the morning, you has to go for a little run! Once round the lake. Get moving – one-two one-two one-two!!'

Janet Perkins and the rest of the trainees set off round the lake. 'Oh ... dear ...' she panted to a woman who was running along beside her. 'This ... is ... rather ... hard work ... don't you think?'

'It certainly ... is,' replied the other sec. 'I work ... at the ... Frank Bruno Church of England ... Mixed Infant School ... But this ... is much ... tougher ... than even that!'

As they came round the far end of the lake, Brigadier Bletherington-Gore and his driver, Bob Wagstaff, were standing in front of his large staff car, which was parked beside the road.

'That's jolly well it, ladies. Keep it up! It'll do you the world of good!'

'Silly old buffer,' thought Janet, 'I bet he couldn't run round a goldfish bowl, let alone a lake!'

Breakfast was a welcome thought. The school secretaries, many of them now rather alarming shades of pink, purple and red, sank down on the dining-hall benches in front of large mugs of tea and plates of egg, bacon, tomatoes, mushrooms and beans.

However, when they looked down at their plates many of their mouths fell open in horror. The eggs were black. The bacon looked like string and the tomatoes, mushrooms and beans all looked as if they'd recently suffered a fairly large nuclear accident.

'What terrible food,' said Janet to the school sec. from the Frank Bruno C. of E. school.

'I know. I thought the food at Frank Bruno's wasn't very good, but this is appalling! What with all this exercise there'll be nothing left

MENU
STODGE
&
CHIPS
BEANS
A LA
GUNGE
SOGGY
SAGO

of me at the end of a week here if I don't get some decent meals. Oh, by the way, my name's Mrs Dickinson. Call me Myrtle,' she added.

When they were walking from the dining-hall and placing their empty trays on the sill of a small serving hatch that led through to the kitchen, Mrs Perkins got something of a shock. Her eyes must have been deceiving her, but for a moment she was almost certain that as she glanced through the hatchway into the large kitchen she had caught sight of the back of a very familiar figure in a dirty apron, complete with a pair of knobbly legs and torn carpet slippers ... But it couldn't have been who she thought it was, especially as the figure seemed to be talking excitedly into a small hand-held mobile telephone ...

Directed by Corporal Hodgkins the school secretaries assembled in a large lecture theatre, facing a huge blackboard with a big map hanging from it.

When they were all ready, Brigadier Bletherington-Gore strode into the room, and addressed them: 'Now then,' he began, 'before I talk about today's events I need to mention what is going to happen tomorrow morning. We'll be going through some special training exercises which involve you working with real school children. For instance, we'll be looking at your riot control techniques, and giving you some hints and tips on how to maintain the upper hand in all conflict situations. Now, in order to do this we need one of you to volunteer to ring your school up and get them to organize a coachload of assorted juniors to be sent here for the day. It's important that they arrive early in the morning. Any offers?'

Janet Perkins put her hand up straight away. She knew Mr Mackintosh would value the chance of getting some of the children out of the school and off his hands for a while.

'I'll arrange it,' she said.

'Jolly good!' said the Brigadier with a beaming smile in her direction. 'Please phone your school sometime before lunch. About twenty of the little blighters should be enough. Now then,' he continued, 'one of the highlights of your week's course here takes place this afternoon and evening. It's a military combat exercise, or manoeuvre, which will test your skill, initiative and courage under pressure – all characteristics, I'm sure you'll agree, that every tip-top school secretary needs!'

Several of them nodded in agreement.

'The exercise will sound comparatively simple. All you will have to do is capture a tank driven by me. I shall start from the heathland well to the south of the camp here . . .' he tapped with a pointer to a spot on the large map. 'And my aim will be to get to the central parade ground here . . . by midnight. Your job is to stop me! You'll all be equipped with paint guns, like this one here.' He held up a revolver, with a short fat barrel. 'It shoots pellets of paint. My tank will have been "captured" if you can hit it on the turret with a jolly good splodge of paint!' He beamed a smile at his audience. 'I must warn you that Corporal Hodgkins and his men will also be part of the exercise, and will not make it easy for you. I think he'll keep you on your toes with some fairly spectacular surprises! Is that right, Corporal?'

'Oh yes, sir!' said the corporal snappily.

'Anyway, ladies, I'm sure you'll agree that developing the skills necessary to capture a tank under adversity will be supremely useful when it comes to getting back to your schools and making sure they run like clockwork! Now, you'll spend the rest of this morning on map reading, camouflage, weapons training and guerrilla warfare tactics. I'm sure you'll find that this afternoon's exercise is one of the most memorable events in your short stay here.'

How right he was.

Chapter Eight

*In which more than one
person gets 'taken out'*

*

In the camp kitchen, when the breakfast things had all been cleared, and the burnt egg and bacon had been scraped off the plates and put in the dustbins, where it belonged, Mrs Gunge stuffed her mobile telephone into the front of her dirty apron, lit a cigarette, and set to work on tasks that are not usually associated with cooking.

For instance: she slid a carving knife into the top of one of her thick woolly socks; tucked a heavy rolling-pin under her ample armpit; stuffed a packet of biscuits and a short piece of rope into her apron pocket; nipped out through the back door of the dining-hall and set off down the drive towards the main gate.

When she got there she found Private Peacock standing at ease beside the red-and-white barrier, his metal helmet secured tightly on his head and his semi-automatic gun slung smartly from one shoulder.

'Good morning, Ducky,' she said. 'I'm the

51

new cook. I was thinking, you sentry blokes must get awfully bored, standing down here all day with nothing to do.'

'It is a bit boring sometimes,' said Private Peacock, still looking straight ahead and trying not to move his face very much.

'I expects you must get a bit hungry sometimes too,' added the Gunge.

'Yes, specially mid-morning,' he replied.

'I thought so. That's why I've brought down a packet of Choco-Crunch biscuits.' She rummaged in her pocket and pulled out the now rather crumpled packet of biscuits. She held them, temptingly, in front of him.

'Yer legs must ache a fair old bit too.'

'Yes, they do.'

'Why don't you sit down round the side here for a minute and have a good old crunch. No one'll see you. I'll look out for anyone.'

Private Peacock had been on gate duty since six o'clock that morning. His legs did indeed ache rather a lot, and he certainly fancied a couple of Choco-Crunch biscuits.

He looked back up the drive towards the camp and looked out over the red-and-white barrier pole into the empty lane. 'OK,' he said. 'Thanks very much.'

He sat down on a small bench at the side of the sentry's guardhouse. 'Corrr,' he said as he did so, 'that's a bit better.'

'Here,' said Mrs Gunge. 'Let me take that heavy great gun off you,' and she slipped the strap off his shoulder. 'And tell you what, why don't you take that silly tin helmet thing off for a minute or two, it must be very hot in there.'

'Yes, it is,' replied Private Peacock, and he pushed the chin strap up in front of his face and removed the helmet.

'That's the way!' said Mrs Gunge, and as she did so she bopped him very smartly on the top of the nut with the rolling-pin that she'd put under her arm for that very purpose.

She dragged the unconscious figure of Private Peacock inside the guardhouse, and releasing his braces, straps and belt, she removed his smart soldier's uniform, leaving him slumped under a table in the middle of the room, dressed only in his underpants.

She bundled up the khaki uniform, tucked it under her arm and picked up the semi-automatic rifle. 'This lot could be useful later,' she said to herself as she did so. Then she punched a number into her mobile phone.

'Hallo?' she said.

'Yes?' said a big hairy voice.

'I've taken out the sentry. I'm just going to open the barrier. Phase one completed.'

'Good, well done,' said the big hairy voice. 'We're on our way.'

As Mrs Gunge strolled back towards the camp kitchen she noticed quite a lot of strange activity. For instance, Corporal Hodgkins and a small group of soldiers were busily digging a trench in a clump of trees quite near the assault course, and other soldiers seemed to be stretching thin wires across some of the smaller footpaths. In the far distance she could hear the unmistakable deep rumble of a tank's engine warming up.

When she got back to the kitchen she stuck the rifle behind the fridge and hid the army uniform. Then she sat down on a stool by the door with a cup of instant coffee. 'It's hard work,' she thought, 'cooking and washing up, and taking out sentries.'

Outside the kitchen, near where Mrs Gunge was sitting, was a short corridor, and on the wall were a row of hooks for coats, and a yellow public payphone.

She was about halfway through her coffee when she heard someone putting coins into the phone and saying: 'Hallo, it's Mrs Perkins. Could I speak to Mr Mackintosh please?'

Mrs Gunge shuffled her stool nearer the door, and cocked her head on one side to make sure she could hear every word of the conversation.

'Hallo, Mrs Perkins, how are you getting on?' asked a voice at the other end of the line.

Mrs Gunge couldn't believe her luck. Looking through the crack in the door she could plainly see Mrs Perkins. She was wearing a running vest and shorts and had a new purple track suit rolled up under one arm.

'Good morning, Head Teacher. Fine, thank you. I've just been in the gym. It's all very interesting – a little exhausting – but very interesting. I'm phoning because we need to borrow some children tomorrow, for some riot control practice and things. Do you think you could send about twenty of the fourth year over, really early in the morning?'

'I'd be delighted, absolutely delighted.' (What with having to run the school single-handed, and having to cook all the food, the idea of getting rid of a coachload of children did indeed fill him with delight.)

'Are you getting on all right?' asked Mrs Perkins brightly.

'I'm just fine,' said Mr Mackintosh, 'but I must go now, there's smoke coming from under the kitchen door.'

'Smoke? That'll be that awful Mrs Gunge. Really! And I asked her to be extra helpful too.'

'Oh it's not her,' exclaimed Mr Mackintosh. 'She left on Friday.'

'Left?'

'Yes, she walked out soon after you'd gone home on Friday. I'm doing the cooking myself. I must go . . . I can see flames.' And there was a click as he put the phone down.

Janet Perkins put the phone back on its hook: 'Mrs Gunge has left . . . How very strange,' said Janet aloud.

'Yes, it is strange, ain't it!' said a rough voice behind her. And a moment later Janet Perkins' arm had been twisted up her back, and an ugly carving knife was being held at her throat!

A few moments after that she had her hands tied behind her back with a short piece of rope.

Then she was pushed across a corridor and through a door that had a small sign on it that said OFFICERS' DINING-ROOM. Like Indiana Jones or James Bond, Mrs Perkins knew that if you are in difficulties the most important thing is to stay alert and attentive, and not to waste time and energy struggling to escape if escape is impossible.

Escape was impossible now, what with her hands tied behind her back, and Mrs Gunge's carving knife not very far from her throat.

So Janet concentrated on her surroundings. She noted the layout of the small room, the position of the small window and of the long sideboard with empty wine glasses on it. In the middle of the room there was a round table covered with a large white table cloth and with knives and forks and a small brass bell on it.

'This is the end of your commando training, Bossy Bum!' said Mrs Gunge with a horrible smirk, and she pushed Janet through another door and into a broom cupboard, where she slumped uncomfortably to the floor. Then, using another length of rope Mrs Gunge tied Janet's legs together tightly, and generally trussed her up so that any movement was well nigh impossible. 'We'll come and release you when we're ready and not before,' she added roughly and with a hideous cackle she shut the cupboard door.

Then she pulled her mobile phone from the front of her pinny and punched in some numbers.

'Hallo, 'Arry,' she said. 'Phase two completed. I've taken out the Perkins woman. She's all trussed up like a Christmas turkey. She won't give you any trouble. All we've got to do now is round up the rest of the secs, and the ransoming can start!'

'Well done,' said Hairy Harry's horrible voice. 'We'll be with you any time now. Stand by for surprises, they won't know what's hit 'em!'

Chapter Nine

*In which Driver Wagstaff
discovers that he's got a problem*

*

Driver Bob Wagstaff had had a very easy sort of morning. He'd got up early, as all good soldiers do, and after giving the Brigadier's staff car a quick going over with a feather duster and checking the tyres and the petrol gauge, he'd set off to collect his lord and master from his house. Then he'd driven him to the edge of the lake, so that the Brigadier could watch the recruits doing their prebreakfast run.

He'd hung around the back of the lecture hall while the school secretaries were briefed on the day's activities, and then he'd driven the brigadier over to a hut on the far side of camp where his tank was being got ready for the impending military exercise.

'It all looks quite satisfactory here, Wagstaff,' said Brigadier Bletherington-Gore, returning to the car with a pleased grin on his face. 'You can take the afternoon orf. I'll get a lift in the Corporal's jeep until the exercise starts.'

'Very good, sir,' said Driver Wagstaff, who liked the idea of an afternoon orf.

Driver Wagstaff got back into the car. 'Now, how shall I start my half-day?' he thought to himself. 'I know, I'll go down to the Crown and Ferret for a glass of lemonade before lunch!'

And that's what he did. It was very pleasant to be in the large swanky car without the brigadier – it made it easy to pretend for the moment that the car was his own, and not the property of Her Majesty's Armed Forces.

It sped down the drive with a satisfactory purr and Bob didn't even have to stop at the guardhouse because the barrier pole was already up.

'Peacock's probably gone to sleep! Lazy blighter,' laughed Driver Wagstaff as he turned out on to the lane.

As you know, he wasn't far wrong.

The Crown and Ferret was a very homely looking pub with black beams, white walls, a red tile roof, and pink roses growing up round the windows. There was a car-park round the side, and on the grass near the front door were a couple of wooden tables with benches beside them, for people and families who liked a drink outside.

Bob Wagstaff parked the car at the side of the pub, locked it carefully, and went inside.

'Good morning, Reg,' he said to the tall thin man behind the bar.

''Morning, Bob. What'll you have?'

'Just a small lemonade please, and a packet of crisps.' Bob sipped his lemonade, quietly, and crunched his crisps, noisily.

But he hadn't been doing it very long before he was joined at the bar by another drinker, who stole up to him in such a silent and stealthy manner that Bob jumped a bit when he spoke: 'Good morning. Nice day.'

'Yes,' said Bob Wagstaff, 'very nice.'

'I see you're in the army then,' said the stranger, his eyes travelling briefly up and down Bob's smart driver's uniform.

'Yes, I am.'

'Fine life for a man! Excellent. Tell you what, can I buy you another drink?'

'Well, just a lemonade then, thank you very much. My name's Bob by the way. Bob Wagstaff. I drive that big army car out there; I'm the Brigadier's chauffeur actually.'

'Excellent,' said the stranger again. 'My name's Nigel. Just Nigel.'

This wasn't strictly true; his full name was Nigel the Nicker!

They chatted for a while, about this and that, and after a short time Bob said: 'Now then, let me buy you a drink this time.'

'Very well, very kind of you, Bob, old chap,' said the Nicker.

Bob Wagstaff put his hands into his deep army uniform trouser pocket and brought out his car keys and a handful of small change. He sorted through the change to find the right amount for two more drinks.

The moment Bob tried to attract the attention of the tall man behind the bar, Nigel the Nicker's hand shot out along the counter and grabbed the car keys. He was as quick as a viper that's spotted a tasty young frog.

'I'm just going to nip to the loo, Bob, back in a tick,' said the Nicker, and he stole quickly and quietly through the door that led to gents' toilet. It also led to the car-park.

Bob Wagstaff sipped his drink alone. Ten minutes passed: there was still no sign of his new drinking friend.

'I don't reckon your pal's coming back,' said the barman.

'That's odd,' replied Bob. 'I'd better go and have a look.'

He drained his glass and went out to the toilet. There was no sign of his new friend there. He walked on through the back door and out into the car-park. There was no sign of his new friend there either.

And neither was there any sign of Brigadier Bletherington-Gore's car!

Chapter Ten

*Most of which we share with Mrs
Perkins, in a broom cupboard*

*

Janet Perkins lay on the floor in the broom
cupboard, and wondered what to do next.

There was quite a good-sized gap under the
door, and although this was the only source
of light in the cupboard, it wasn't long before
her eyes became accustomed to the semi-
darkness, and she was able to make out some
of the things that surrounded her.

There were mops and brooms and a couple
of buckets, and high up on the walls, way out
of her reach, were shelves with boxes on
them. Janet wriggled until she was flat on
her back and then strained her eyes trying to
make out any lettering on the side of the
boxes which could give her a clue as to what
might be inside them, but it was too dark to
see. Maybe they contained wine bottles.

'This is obviously where the catering staff
keep their cleaning things and spare supplies
for the officers' dining-room that I came
through,' she said to herself.

Then she noticed that at the far end of one

of the shelves there was a stack of dinner plates. She could just make them out in the gloom.

Suddenly a wry smile played on Mrs Perkins' lips – or it would have done if the gag that Mrs Gunge had made out of a dishcloth hadn't got in the way.

66

She was very tightly tied up, and the ropes hurt her wrists and legs. But ignoring the pain as much as she could, she began to wriggle and twist and struggle in an attempt to move towards one of the brooms.

After much heaving and panting, she twisted herself round so that she was sitting up with the broom behind her. Although her wrists were tightly tied she could just manage to get her hands round the handle of the broom.

After much more struggling she managed to position herself, with the broom safely in her hands behind her, to the spot on the floor that was directly below the pile of plates on the shelf.

With steely determination in her eyes, and a pounding heart inside her running vest, she set about the tricky task of using the broom to knock just one plate off the shelf. 'If they all come down,' she said to herself, 'the noise will attract attention and I'll be sunk.'

The job was incredibly difficult, not just because she was working in darkness, but also because of the ropes that bit into her, and the fact that the broom was behind her back and only just long enough to reach the plates.

But Mrs Perkins, as you will know, is a bit like Robert the Bruce's spider. She's not the sort of person who gives up. And after an hour or so of trying and then trying again she'd got the top plate well out on its own, teetering precariously.

With a crash it fell to the floor. As she had hoped, it broke into at least three pieces, and one of them was just within her reach.

Shuffling on her bottom she managed to get to it, and then began the long process of using a fragment of broken crockery to cut through the rope that bound her wrists.

The broken china was very sharp, and, relying as she had to on only her sense of touch, she had to be very careful that she didn't accidentally cut her wrists.

By the time her hands were free, her arms ached terribly. She lent with her back resting against the door, and waited to regain her strength.

'I don't know . . .' she said eventually, out loud, 'a school secretary's life has a lot more adventure and variety in it than most people imagine.' She gave a tired sigh. 'I suppose it must be nearly going-home time at St Gertrude's, and here am I getting tied up and put in cupboards when I should be thinking about capturing tanks! I wonder how poor Mr Mackintosh is getting on . . .'

Actually, back at St Gertrude's, Mr Mackintosh was taking an Assembly in the school hall, before releasing the children into the outside world at the end of the day. In fact he was making an announcement.

All Mr Mackintosh's announcements were important (all Head Teachers' announcements are) but this one, although he did not know it at the time, would have a serious and dramatic effect on the whole history of St Gertrude's school:

'Now, settle down and listen carefully,' he began. 'You all know that Mrs Perkins has gone off to a military training camp that helps to revitalize school secretaries. Well, tomorrow the children in Mrs Patel's class will be going to the camp to help with some riot control training exercises. So will they come and see me after Assembly to collect notes for their parents. I will be driving the bus, and we'll leave from the school gate at eight o'clock in the morning. It's very important that no one is late. Understand?'

The children in Mrs Patel's class, including Billy Baxter, Belinda Bollard, Yashpal Singh, Sandra Jarrett, Wes Richards and other friends whom you may have read about before, nodded and said 'yes'. They gave each other excited glances. It certainly sounded as if they were in for an unusual day tomorrow.

How right they were . . .

Chapter Eleven

*During which we attend a very
interesting tea party*

*

With one bound Mrs Janet Perkins was free
from the broom cupboard.

'The sooner I get some sensible clothes on,
and can find out what's going on around here,
the better,' she said to herself as she shut the
cupboard door behind her and started off
across the officers' dining-room.

She'd only taken about three steps towards
the door when she heard something that sent
a shock of horror through her sturdy frame.
Someone was coming into the room! Almost
as if it was happening in slow motion, she
saw the handle of the door that led to her
freedom, turning. She heard gruff, masculine
voices.

With the speed of a cheetah, or a school
secretary who senses that danger is nigh, she
dived on to the floor and rolled skilfully
under the table. If a trained commando had
been there to see it he would have given her
a round of applause. But luckily for her no
one saw her, and no one could see her now,

as she crouched beneath the dining-room's round table, well-concealed by the overhanging white table-cloth.

Then she heard a voice that she instantly recognized.

'Jolly well come in, chaps!' said Brigadier Bletherington-Gore cheerfully. She could tell from his voice that he was very pleased with himself. 'Sit where you like, men. I thought I'd take the opportunity of meeting you all in here for a bit of tea before tonight's exercise starts. I've got some rather exciting secret information for you!'

Janet held her breath and tried to be as thin as possible, as six sets of legs in army trousers and twelve very shiny black army boots, shuffled into position all round her. She knew that if she could stay concealed under the table without being discovered, she might learn some vital information about the enemy's plans! In common with anyone who works in schools she knew the value of careful spywork, or espionage. She took the whole subject very seriously.

'OK, Corporal?' said the Brigadier, when the men all seemed settled into position.

'Yes, SIR!' snapped the Corporal in a voice so loud it was all Janet Perkins could do not to jerk her head up and hit it on the underside of the table.

'Jolly good.' He rang the small brass bell that Janet had noticed on the table during her rapid journey through the room earlier in the day.

Janet heard the door open, and in shuffled Mrs Gunge. You could almost catch the smell of rotting school cabbage.

'Ah!' said the Brigadier. 'Yes, we're ready for tea now, my dear, if you'd be so kind.'

'OK, Boss,' grumbled Gunge, and Janet could hear the rattle of cups and saucers as a large trolley was wheeled in and things were put on the table.

'Are the school secretaries assembled for their tea yet?' The Brigadier was obviously speaking to Mrs Gunge.

'Yea, they're just coming into the dining-hall now.'

'Good show! Make sure they get plenty of food, they're in for a busy night!' And he chuckled a rather mischievous chuckle.

Mrs Gunge left the room and the door closed behind her. When he was sure that she'd gone the Brigadier spoke in a voice that was quiet enough not to carry through the door and out of the room. Janet Perkins had no difficulty hearing every word.

'Now, chaps,' he began. 'We've got a rather fiendish new toy which I'm going to introduce into tonight's exercise.'

Janet could almost hear his self-satisfied smile.

'You know that the secretaries have got to zap my tank with their paint-pellet guns. Well, we're introducing a rather fascinating decoy into the proceedings.'

'Decoy, sir?' asked one of the soldiers. 'Isn't that some kind of duck?'

'Not exactly,' replied the Brigadier. 'The

essence of a decoy, is that it's a fake. Decoys deceive people – or ducks. Our decoy is a fake *tank*, and it's jolly well going to deceive our little friends, the school secretaries.'

'How will it work, sir?' snapped Corporal Hodgkins. Janet recognized his voice.

'Well, that's the clever bit. You see, I'll be in my tank. It's been painted black and we've fitted extra silencers to it, so it'll be pretty tricky to spot on a dark night like tonight. But we've got an unmanned second tank, a decoy, that's stuffed to the tin lid with flares and explosives. I shall direct it by remote control from my own driving position, and I shall send it through the woods about two hundred metres ahead of me. It makes quite a lot of noise and has small side lights that I can turn on, so any good school sec. will spot it in no time. The idea is that while they concentrate on the decoy, I slip past them and make a dash for the central parade ground.

'Please, sir, won't they realize it's a fake when they get close to it?' asked a soldier's voice.

'Ah ha! Now here's the really clever bit. I told you that the decoy is filled to the gutters with flares and explosives. Well, the outside of it is covered with small detonator pads!'

Janet could tell from the way that the room

went silent for a moment and the soldiers' boots shuffled in embarrassment, that the Brigadier's audience was still not quite clear what he was talking about.

He helped them out: 'When the secs spot the decoy tank they'll try to zap it with paint pellets. The moment a pellet hits one of the detonators on the outside of the tank the whole thing explodes and disappears before their eyes in a blinding flash of light! They'll be so confused and mystified by the whole bally thing that it's a total doddle for me to slip past the poor old dears!'

'"Poor old dears" indeed!' Mrs Perkins, under the table, could feel herself become red, angry and very determined (a dangerous condition in a school secretary).

'You and your men, Corporal,' continued the triumphant Brigadier, 'will be deployed in a trench near the assault course. Early in the night I need you to create plenty of excitement for the secs, to keep them on their toes. Use the usual trip-wire flares etc. OK?'

'OK, sir.'

'Right, men. I think you can now disperse to your positions and I'll go and get into my command tank. I must say I'm rather looking forward to tonight's fun and games. I haven't played around with a radio-controlled vehicle since I was a lad at Prep school!'

Chairs were pushed back, army boots withdrew from her sight and Mrs Janet Perkins breathed a sigh of relief. Even though she was dressed only in running shorts and T-shirt, beads of apprehensive sweat had broken out on her brow.

The door closed. The room fell silent and empty. 'Time for me to go into action!' said Janet through clenched teeth. 'They won't know what's hit them!'

She stood up and was just about to begin the next stage of her escape when something that had been stuffed under the dining-room's sideboard earlier in the day, caught her eye . . .

Chapter Twelve

Oh dear, Mrs Gunge goes into action

*

Mrs Perkins wasn't the only person that tea-time who was listening in to what other people were saying.

Out in the commando camp dining-hall Mrs Gunge was shuffling between the tables, dishing out burnt bits of toast, and huge spoonfuls of lukewarm baked beans, and while she did it she kept an ear out for any interesting bits of information. As you know, this is called espionage.

'I wonder where that nice Mrs Perkins has got to?' said one voice.

'I don't know,' said another.

'Perhaps she's had to go back to her school or something. You know what it is when duty calls,' added a third.

'It's a pity though, I thought she would be very useful to lead us through tonight's tank-capturing exercise.' The speaker was Myrtle Dickinson.

Mrs Gunge made sure she could hear every word of the following discussion:

'Maybe you should take charge, Myrtle, in

Mrs Perkins' absence?'

'Yes, please do, I think we'll need a leader.'

'Perhaps we should all have a meeting in our dormitory to discuss tactics before we start the exercise?'

Myrtle Dickinson, from the Frank Bruno C. of E. Infants School, stood up. Mrs Gunge sidled out into her kitchen, but the moment she was there she dashed round to the serving hatch to listen, a ghastly grin of impending triumph on her face.

'Ladies!' said Mrs Dickinson firmly. 'On this table we feel that it would be a good idea if we all had a get-together before tonight's exercise starts, so that we can elect a leader, and discuss our tactics. Do you agree?'

Lots of the school secretaries made it clear that they agreed:

'Good idea, Myrtle.'

'Great!'

'Of course!'

'Right then,' said Mrs Dickinson, assuming control – as she often had to at Frank Bruno's – let's all gather together in our dormitory in ten minutes. We must make sure that we are not overheard, and that there are no strangers around. Agreed?'

'Yes!' said the secretaries.

'By the way,' added Mrs Dickinson, 'do keep a look out for Mrs Perkins from St

Gertrude's; no one seems to know where she's gone. I'd hate her to miss the night's exercise. I'm sure she'd be rather good at tank capturing.'

Mrs Gunge, at the serving hatch, had a job to restrain a witch-like cackly laugh!

The school secretaries got up from their tables and began to make their way out of the dining-room.

Mrs Gunge leant on one of the filthy kitchen surfaces and rubbed her whiskery chin in deep thought. 'Now, how the devil can I get in on their meeting?'

As she was thinking this her eyes just happened to be attracted to a bundle lying on the chair by the telephone, just outside the kitchen door.

It was Mrs Perkins' purple track suit, left there when she'd been kidnapped earlier in the day. Almost as soon as Mrs Gunge spotted it, a gigantic idea struck her. It caused her piggy little eyes to widen and her greasy jaw to drop open. 'CORRRR!' she said to herself: 'Wait a bit! That's it! That's blinking blooming blumming well IT!!!! MRS BOSSY BUM PERKINS IS GOIN' TO MAKE A DRAMATIC REAPPEARANCE!!'

How right she was, whatever she meant . . .

Mrs Gunge swept the track suit up under her arm, took a candle, a box of matches and the cork from a wine bottle out of the kitchen drawer, and went off into the cook's lavatory. Come, we will follow her. . .

After quite a lot of struggling and straining, Mrs Gunge managed to get into Mrs Perkin's lovely new purple track suit. It didn't look all that lovely on her – in fact it looked pretty terrible.

. . .

Then she stood the candle beside the grubby wash-basin, and lit it. She then held the cork in the flame until it smouldered and turned black.

Using the blackened cork like an infant's black crayon, she covered her face in black stripes and smudges. By the time she'd added her old woollen balaclava from the hook behind the loo door and had tied a filthy grey tea-towel over her face, highwayman-style, she looked quite like something from the top commando unit of the SAS.

'This'll fox them! Silly moos!' she said to herself with a grin. Then, picking up Private Peacock's semi-automatic rifle from behind the fridge, where she'd hidden it, she waddled off towards the school secretaries' dormitory, and the next stage of her fiendish plan.

Chapter Thirteen

*In which night falls, and several
people are up to no good!*

*

When Mrs Perkins crept out of the officers'
dining-room a few seconds later, she did not
notice that her new purple track suit was no
longer lying on the chair by the telephone,
just outside the kitchen door, where she had
left it.

The reason she didn't notice its absence
was simple: she no longer needed it. And the
reason she no longer needed it was because
the thing she'd spotted stuffed under the sideboard at the end of chapter eleven was Private Peacock's army uniform!

It didn't take Mrs Perkins very long to put
the uniform on and by the time she'd added
the tin helmet, she, too, looked quite
SASish.

She feared that the terrible Mrs Gunge
might still be lurking in the kitchen area, so
she opened the officers' dining-room door as
silently as possible and then flattened herself,
as best she could, against the wall in the
corridor. She tiptoed towards the kitchen

door, and checking that no one was around, peered into the kitchen.

Good, it seemed to be empty.

Then she noticed something interesting lying by one of the large kitchen sinks. It was Mrs Gunge's portable telephone. 'Right, I think that might come in useful,' said Mrs Perkins, and she grabbed it and stuffed it into the pocket in her army uniform trousers.

When she opened the back door and slipped silently out into the camp grounds she was quite surprised at how dark it had become. She darted, like a forest deer at twilight, between the shadowy shapes of huts and trees.

Suddenly the lights of a large army car swung across her path. She dived for cover into a small bush and crouched low, holding her breath. 'Good, they didn't see me,' she said to herself as she lay in the bush getting her breath back. 'I think I'll stay put here for a moment and await developments.'

(Robin Hood would probably have done the same thing.)

It was indeed fortunate that she hadn't been seen by the driver of the car, because it was none other than the Nicker, and the car contained Hairy Harry the Hatchet Man, Cracker Crawford, and Hans Zupp.

The car sped past the bush that concealed Mrs Perkins, and went on up the drive.

Before it had gone much further, however, it veered off into the woods, down a small Tarmac drive that led to the southern portion of the camp.

About a mile down this track the car pulled off the road and stopped. Hans Zupp got out, and so did Hairy Harry. They went to the back of the car and opened the boot. From it they took a couple of small oil drums and some red lamps. From the roof of the car they untied several red-and-white wooden poles.

The Nicker then passed them out a sign that said 'HALT! ROAD WORKS.' (He'd nicked it from some council workmen that afternoon.)

'OK, Boss?' he asked as he did so.

'Yea,' said Harry. 'Hans, stay here with me. We'll see you two later.' The car doors were shut, and the Brigadier's large staff car, with the Nicker and Cracker inside it, purred off into the moonlit woods.

Hairy Harry and Hans Zupp started to set up the poles, drums and lamps. In less than ten minutes they had erected a very convincing road works. It was surrounded by dim red lights that glowed in the dark.

'All we gotter do now, Hans,' said Harry slowly, 'is wait. It's a bit like being a spider waiting to catch a fly!'

He fingered the sharp edge of his hatchet as he said it.

Chapter Fourteen

*In which Mrs Gunge makes a
strange request and the school
secs' military exercise gets off
to a very unpromising start*

*

When we last heard of ghastly Mrs Gunge,
she was waddling towards the school secretaries' dormitory wearing Mrs Perkins'
purple track suit, and her face was blackened
with burnt cork and masked with an old tea-
towel. You will also recall that she was carrying a highly dangerous semi-automatic rifle.

Now she knocked on the door of the long
low hut where the school secretaries were
housed. A face looked out through one of the
windows; Mrs Gunge could hear raised, excited voices as the word went round that Mrs
Perkins had returned and was at the door!
The Gunge plan was working, no problem.

A key turned in the lock. It was a sound
that pleased Mrs Gunge immensely (you'll find
out why in a moment) and then she was wel-
comed inside: 'Oh, well done, Mrs Perkins!'

'How splendid – you look just like some
sort of commando!'

'Wherever have you been, my dear?'

'You're just the person we need.'

'Come in, come in!'

She went in.

They were all obviously very pleased to see her. 'Are you all right, Janet?' asked Myrtle Dickinson in a kindly voice. 'We've been quite worried about you!'

'I'm fine,' replied Mrs Gunge in the poshest way she could. Fortunately for her the tea-towel mask helped to disguise her voice as well as her face. 'I've been busy. Carry on with the meeting. I'll go and have a rest at the back here.'

She went to the back of the room and sat down on a chair.

'Right then, ladies!' called out Myrtle Dickinson, in a school-teachery voice. 'Let's continue our meeting.' She got up on a chair, and the other school secretaries gathered round her in a semicircle. 'I'm sure,' she said, 'that the soldiers here will try to spring a lot of surprises on us, just as children try to at school! But I'm sure we'll be up to any little tricks that are thrown our way. (Mrs Gunge smiled at this – under the tea-towel.) 'As you know, the important thing is that we keep calm and think clearly, even when the going gets rough.'

The school secretaries murmured their agreement.

'I think it will be best if we split into small groups; that way if some of us get taken out by enemy action, the others can continue the search for the tank. I've taken the liberty of appointing ten of us to lead these small patrols.'

She read out the names of ten patrol leaders, all of whom agreed to accept the responsibilities of their important new roles.

'I also think it will be sensible if we darken our faces, as clever Mrs Perkins has done. It will make us much more difficult to be spotted in the dark.' They all turned and smiled with admiration at the person they thought was Janet Perkins. Mrs Gunge gave a grin, but again, thanks to the grubby tea-towel, none of them could see it.

'Now, before we finally get ready, are there any questions?' asked Mrs Dickinson.

No one had any questions.

'No? Any requests?'

'YES!' said Mrs Gunge standing up at the back of the room. 'I've got a request.'

'What is it, Mrs Perkins, dear?' asked Myrtle Dickinson.

'I request,' said Mrs Gunge with a snarl, 'THAT YOU ALL STICK YER HANDS UP!' And she pulled the tea-towel from her face, and produced Private Peacock's semi-automatic rifle from behind her back!

To say that the school secretaries were surprised would be an understatement. They were totally and absolutely dumbfounded and stunned! Their mouths dropped open. One or two of them sank down on to beds and chairs. Some uttered tiny cries of horror and disbelief.

'Come on, come on! Don't just stand there like a lot of cows what's backed into a 'lectric fence! GET YER 'ANS UP!' snarled Mrs Gunge again, in her nastiest voice. (Hans Zupp would have been proud of her.)

Slowly a small forest of bewildered school secretaries' hands crept ceilingwards. 'We th ... th ... thought ...' stammered Mrs Dickinson almost in a whisper. 'We thought ... that you were Mrs Perkins ...'

'Well you thought wrong, didn't yer!' said Mrs Gunge triumphantly. 'If you really wanna know, Mrs Blooming Perkins is trussed up, right now, like a steak and kidney pudding in my broom cupboard!'

(We know that this was not strictly true. Mrs Perkins was, at that moment, resting in a rhododendron bush in the camp grounds collecting her thoughts. But we'll let Mrs Gunge continue uncorrected ...)

'So yer all done for!'

'But ...' said one of the secretaries, her voice quivering on the edge of tears, 'does this mean that we've failed the military manoeuvre before it's even started?'

'Military remover! Military remover? I don't know anythink about your military remover! What I know is that you lot is kidnapped! Kidnapped good and proper,' said Mrs Gunge.

She strode over to the door and turned the large key in the lock. She held it up triumphantly in one hand, her other rested on the trigger of her rifle. 'I suggest you all gets down on the floor, and gets some sleep! Tomorra' morning, when a few good friends of mine have taken care of the stupid Brigadier and his silly soldiers, we'll be sending ransom notes with your names on to some pretty important people! We reckon you lot is worth a tidy little sum! Ha!' she sneered venomously. 'You're all going to make my fortune!'

And she tucked the large key out of sight down the front of her track suit.

'What if the important people won't pay up?' asked a school secretary apprehensively.

'Well,' said Mrs Gunge, 'that's easy. I SHOOTS YOU!'

A light breeze ruffled through the room as fifty school secretaries drew breath at this terrible thought.

'Now get down on the floor, and shut up!'

said Mrs Gunge, sweeping the hideous black gun across them so that it momentarily pointed at each secretary in turn. 'Any trouble and I'll fill you with more lead than a box of school pencils!'

The secretaries sank to the floor. There was a look of abject misery on every face.

'To think ...' thought Mrs Dickinson, 'I came here to be rejuvenated and instead I've been hijacked by a greasy dinner lady who threatens to shoot me. If only Janet Perkins was here ... If only ...'

Chapter Fifteen

The green flare goes up.
Let battle commence!

*

Corporal Hodgkins, in his jeep, had already taken Brigadier Bletherington-Gore to a secret location at the southern tip of the camp where his tank was hidden.

It was a mighty black beast, with thick steel sides, and was covered in rows of rivets – like the spots on a teenager's chin.

'Help me up, Corporal, there's a good chappie!' said the Brigadier, and the Corporal and a couple of his soldiers gave their commanding officer's large backside a push and a shove to help him on his way up to the tank's large turret, and the hatch that led down into its metallic interior.

As you know, Brigadier Bletherington-Gore is a rather rotund man, roughly the shape of a football, only much bigger, and it was quite a while before he'd squeezed himself down into the tank driver's seat, which was positioned low down at the front, just under the big rotatable gun turret.

He raised the heavy metal flap that opened

a slit for him to look out of the tank.

'Very good, Corporal. I think everything is in order. I suggest you fire the green flare to signal that the night exercise has commenced!'

Corporal Hodgkins went over to his jeep, which was parked nearby, and took a flare pistol from an ammunition compartment at the back. He raised its fat barrel in the air and pulled the trigger. A flare rocket snaked its way into the night sky, and burst overhead in a shower of Kermit-green light.

Inside the tank the Brigadier flicked several switches, checked some gauges and pressed the starter button that sent its mas-

sive engine into life with a deep rumbling purr. 'Good, the extra silencers seem to be doing their work,' he said to himself.

The Brigadier really enjoyed military manoeuvres. He'd been in one or two small wars since joining the army, but he hadn't enjoyed them at all. Indeed, he hadn't joined the army in the first place in order to either kill people or get killed himself. He'd joined because he liked the company of men, and machines, and he'd thought that work in an office or factory would be a bit boring. Military exercises were just right: they gave him lots of excitement without any danger.

He sat now, deep in the innards of the tank.

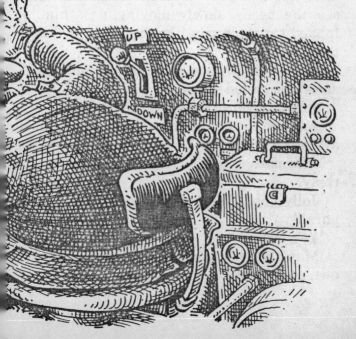

He was, of course, familiar with the levers and handles that operated it, but tonight, at his right-hand side, was a small box of new and intriguing controls, a small joy stick and a row of about six switches. 'Ah!' thought the Brigadier. 'I can't wait to see how the remote control decoy works! It should be a lot of jolly good fun!'

He eased the stick forward. A small TV monitor and rows of red lights suggested that the new decoy was on the move. 'Can you see the decoy tank, Corporal? Is it operational?' called the Brigadier through the driver's slit.

'Affirmative, sir!' shouted Corporal Hodgkins, and a moment later the Brigadier could see the decoy slowly moving past him. It looked satisfactorily like any other ordinary tank.

'Is it well primed with flares and explosives?' he called again.

'Affirmative, sir!' replied the Corporal.

'And are the percussion detonators in place all over it?'

'Affirmative, sir!' called the Corporal in reply.

'Jolly good! Well off we go to battle, Corporal!'

'Yes, sir!'

'May the best team win! Disperse to your own positions!'

'Yes, sir! Very good, sir!'

As the Corporal's jeep sped off down a small track that led by a roundabout route to the centre of the camp, Brigadier Bletherington-Gore eased his mighty tank forward across the heath towards the wooded parkland of the army camp.

For the first half mile or so he was so busy driving his own tank, and directing the decoy a few metres ahead of him that he didn't even think about the chance of being spotted or zapped by the enemy. It would in any case be highly unlikely that they would have reached that far south already; so he just concentrated on driving. He came to a small Tarmac track, and checked on his map that he needed to follow it for a few hundred metres before cutting left into the woods.

What with his double driving task, and a bit of map reading, his mind was well occupied.

It was quite a shock to him therefore when he came round the end of a small copse and was confronted with a row of red lights and a red-and-white sign in the middle of some poles that said 'HALT! ROAD WORKS'.

'What the blithering blazes???' he said out loud, pulling on the tank's brake lever, and putting the decoy's joy stick into its neutral position.

As the large tank and its accompanying decoy came to a halt, a figure emerged from a small workman's tent that was made from red-and-white striped plastic. The Brigadier was not slow to shout at him: 'Now look here, my man! What the bally heck is going on? I'm in the middle of a very important military exercise, designed to toughen up some of the nation's crack troops. Why wasn't I told about these ridiculous road works?'

'Oh,' said the man, who wasn't a workman at all, but Hans Zupp. 'Well, you see, it's an emergency. A water main has busted. We've got to get it fixed.'

'Well, how can I get past you? This isn't a Dinky toy you know!'

'Tell you what,' said Hans in a helpful tone of voice. 'I'll move a few of the poles and things, and we'll let you through. It won't take a moment, sir.'

'Well I say, that's jolly decent of you,' replied the Brigadier, pleased that the man had come round to his way of thinking so quickly.

What Brigadier Bletherington-Gore didn't know was that, while he was having his little conversation with our friend Hans Zupp, and winning him round so easily, a second figure was climbing on to the back of his tank.

By the time Hans had managed to move a

couple of the red-and-white poles and the halt sign, this second figure was on the top of the tank's gun turret.

By the time the small red lamps had been shifted, and the way was clear for the tank and its decoy to proceed, this second figure had managed to lift up the metal lid on the top of the tank, and with some difficulty – for rather like the Brigadier he too was a large man – he had slid down silently inside the mighty machine.

'Is all clear?' called the Brigadier to his new-found friend the road mender.

'Yer, I think you'll get past no bother now,' called back Hans.

'I very much appreciate your cooperation, old sport,' said the Brigadier. 'I'll get on with my military manoeuvre!'

He touched the tank's throttle and the engine gave a muffled roar. He was just about to engage first gear and ease forward, when an arm went round his neck, threatening to strangle him, and a rough voice snarled: 'Not so fast, fatso . . .'

You may not need me to tell you that the arm round the Brigadier's neck was quite remarkably big and hairy!

Chapter Sixteen

*In which Mrs Perkins learns a lot,
just by sitting and listening*

*

A long way off, in a rhododendron bush not far from the heart of the camp, Mrs Perkins was watching, listening and thinking.

By now the night was deep and still. Only the lightest of winds ruffled the topmost branches of the tall trees that dotted the spaces between the camp buildings and roads.

When the moon emerged from a high cloud, Janet could see her surroundings quite clearly – her night vision was excellent, especially with her long-distance glasses.

The sudden hoot of a screech owl made her jump and set her heart racing inside her army tunic.

'I wonder if I should make a move?' she thought to herself. 'This damp little bush can't be doing my rheumatism any good.'

If only she could be sure what was going on. Mrs Gunge was obviously up to something very suspicious, if not deadly, but where were all the school secretaries? An hour or two earlier she'd seen the green flare rocketing its way into the sky, so she knew that in theory the exercise had started, so where was everybody? Why was it all so quiet?

She was pondering this when she saw lights approaching through the distant trees. They belonged to a vehicle, but from this far away she couldn't be sure what type.

She crouched lower, like a tiger that thinks it may have spotted its lunch but can't be sure. Soon she could make it out. It was an army jeep, and it was full of soldiers.

The jeep came to a halt only a few metres from her and its occupants spoke in voices that she remembered from her spell under the dining-room table earlier in the day.

'OK, you guys!' said Corporal Hodgkins. 'Get moving!'

Janet could see four or five other men tumbling out of the back of the jeep and lining up beside it.

'Now,' said the Corporal. 'We're in line with the path the Brigadier's tank and its decoy will take, so it's highly likely that some of the school secs may try to intercept it in this region. We're here to give them a few little surprises, like. Understand?'

The soldiers seemed to indicate that they understood.

'We're going to sit in this trench, here,' continued the Corporal. 'I've set trip-wires which set off mock grenades between all the trees over there to the north. The old dears will probably come from that direction, so that should give them a few heart attacks!'

The little group of soldiers guffawed at this, and Janet's fists tightened as she heard it.

'Also, in the trench we've got stun grenades, firecrackers, rocket flares – just about everything from Roman candles to Catherine wheels! The minute we hunch any secs may be in danger of zapping the Brig's tanks, we'll let them have it with a few rather sophisticated fireworks. It's what we in the army call "creating a diversion". We'll create so many diversions they'll probably wet themselves!'

'Ha Ha Ha!' went the soldiers.

Janet Perkins went red, and then white, with indignation. 'Stupid men! Just you wait!!' she said between clenched dentures.

Luckily the moon slid into quite a large area of clear sky, and Janet watched intently as she saw the soldiers carry ammunition boxes from the back of the jeep.

Then, while one of them parked the vehicle out of sight, the others jumped down into the trench, taking the boxes with them.

Then all went quiet. 'Keep your eyes skinned, lads,' Janet heard the Corporal remark: 'We just sit and wait – like a spider waiting to catch a fly!'

Janet Perkin's mind began to race. If only she could neutralize the danger these soldiers posed to the gallant secretaries. If only she could get her hands on some of their ammo, maybe she could capture the tank on her own? One way or another she knew she wanted to teach a few people a lesson they wouldn't forget in a hurry!

She hadn't been thinking about these things for very long when she was surprised by another set of lights coming through the trees.

They were approaching from the north,

from behind the trench, and so were unlikely to have been seen by the soldiers inside it.

They were car lights, and by the time the vehicle had coasted to a halt in the middle distance Janet had no difficulty in recognizing whose car it was. It was the army car she'd seen that morning, driven by Bob Wagstaff and belonging to the Brigadier.

'That's strange,' she thought. 'The Brigadier's supposed to be in his tank, not inspecting troops here . . .'

It was even stranger, she thought, that the two people who emerged from the large car were not even soldiers. They were civilians, and pretty shady looking civilians at that!

She watched, mesmerized, as she saw them get out of the car, point towards the trench full of soldiers, and then plunge off into the bushes. There was just enough moonlight for Janet to see what the two men were doing.

They were taking a huge rope net down from some posts on the assault course that ran beside the road, not far from where they were parked.

'It's one of those nets that people have to climb on the Krypton Factor,' said Janet to herself. 'A bit like the rigging on an old ship.'

Unfortunately she was too far away to hear what the two men were saying, but if she'd been closer she'd have heard one of them whisper: 'This net'll do the trick, Nicker old boy,' and the other reply: 'It'll be like a spider, Cracker, a spider catching flies!'

She was amazed by what happened next. The two men, dragging the net between them, crept up to the trenchful of soldiers. Like Roman gladiators they threw the net over the trench. Janet heard the stifled shouts of the surprised soldiers. She heard quite a few swear words too – but she was used to hearing them at school.

Then, while one of the men drew the ends of the net together with a rope, the other one ran back to the car and backed it up to the trench!

They tied what was now a struggling ball of soldiers' arms and legs held in a huge string bag, to the back bumper of the Brigadier's car. 'Come on, my beauties!' said Cracker Crawford loudly. 'We don't want you around for a little while, so we're taking you for what may be a rather bumpy ride!'

Janet Perkins put her hand over her mouth in disbelief as the car started up, and the mighty string bag, full of struggling soldiers, was hauled up out of the trench. Then it was dragged, cursing, into the midnight woods!

Janet was even more amazed when Mrs

Gunge's portable telephone, which she had put in her trouser pocket, suddenly rang!

Thinking quickly, as all great heroes do, she pulled it out, switched it on, and in a voice as much like Mrs Gunge's as she could manage, she said, 'Yea?'

''That you, Mrs Gunge?' said the telephone.

'Yea,' said Janet again, in her Gungey voice (sometimes even school secretaries have to tell lies).

'Good. It's 'Arry 'ere. We've captured the Brigadier and 'is stupid tank. I'm sending Hans off to shut the main gates and man the guardhouse so that no busybodies can get through when it gets light, and I'll phone Cracker and Nicker in the car in a tick, to see that they've rounded up those daft soldiers. Then all we need to do is collect up the secs, and the ransoming can start! Ha! Ha! I'll phone yer again, ta-ta for now.'

With a click the phone went silent.

Janet Perkins could not believe her ears!

Chapter Seventeen

While some people are hard at
work – much of the world sleeps

*

Hairy Harry the Hatchet Man was having a happy time. He was driving Brigadier Bletherington-Gore's tank. Harry had never driven a tank before, and he was finding it most enjoyable.

Brigadier Bletherington-Gore was not finding it at all enjoyable. This was because he was lying at the rear of the tank in a dark and greasy locker which would have held the tank's ammunition if they had been going into real war. It felt a bit like real war to the Brigadier, only a lot worse.

Harry swung round and shouted to him: 'Hey, fatso! What's the number of the phone in your car?'

'453671,' replied the Brigadier. 'Why?'

''Cos I want to phone my little friends, and they happen to be in your car, that's why!'

'Blooming damn cheek!' said the Brigadier. He had a red face at normal times – now he looked like a Dayglo beetroot.

'Shut up!' said Harry. 'Or I'll be forced to

do a bit of hatchet practice, and that would interrupt my driving!'

Harry was actually getting quite good at driving the tank. He'd soon found the accelerator and brake, and in no time he got the hang of pulling the levers which made the enormous machine turn left or right.

There were of course a lot of controls that he simply ignored – especially those concerned with firing the gun and turning the turret. He also took no notice of a small joy stick, rather like the one you'd use to direct a remote-controlled toy car, which was situated very close to his right elbow. Not only did he ignore it, he didn't even notice it was there, or that he kept nudging it with his large hairy elbow. Later on in the night he probably wished he had been slightly more careful about it.

He took out his phone and jabbed in the Brigadier's car phone number with his hairy banana fingers.

'Hallo,' said a voice answering on the other end.

'Is that you, Cracker?' asked Harry.

'Yes!' said Cracker, for indeed it was.

'Good,' said Harry. 'I'm in the Brigadier's tank. He's locked up in the back, and I've just spoken to Gungey to tell 'er to look out for secs. Have you taken out the other soldiers like I told you?'

'We certainly have, old boy,' said Cracker with a jolly smile. 'Nicker and I have got them tied to the back of the car in a rope net that he nicked off the assault course. They're as safe as trout in a fisherman's keep-net!'

'Good,' said Harry. 'I'll drive into the camp, and hopefully the secs will see me and attack.

Then we nab 'em and round 'em up in one of the huts. I've sent Hans down to the front gates to shut them. By the morning I reckon the ransoming can start – and I haven't even had to swing me axe yet. It's going to be a doddle! Ta-ta.'

'Toodle-pip, old bean!' said Cracker, replacing the Brigadier's car phone in its rest. 'It's going to be a piece of cake, Nicker, a piece of cake.' He and Nigel the Nicker smiled contentedly at one another, as crooks who sense that things are going their way often do.

Hans Zupp had been instructed by Hairy Harry to go down to the camp's main gate and 'secure' it.

'Lock it up good an' tight, Hans and stay in the guardhouse so that no one can get in. We don't want police or army reinforcements interrupting us while we're doing our delicate negotiations to get millions of quid for all those school secretaries!'

'OK, Boss,' said Hans, and while Harry went off in the Brigadier's tank, Hans started to walk towards the gate as directed.

Hans hadn't realized how very dark the night was, particularly when the moon went behind a cloud, or he was walking through the smalls clumps of trees and bushes that filled so much of the large grounds.

At times he almost bumped into trees – not seeing them until he was nearly upon them. Once he nearly walked into a small lake that he hadn't spotted.

After a mile or so he came out on to the main drive. 'Cor, at last. It should be easy from here,' he said to himself, turning left and walking down the drive. He tried not to let his boots make too much noise on the gravel as he went.

He was quite tired when, a while later, he turned a bend and could just make out the white guardhouse by the side of the main gate. It was still some way off and by the light of the intermittent moon it looked silent and rather ghostly.

Hans felt a small shudder run up his back. 'Creeping about on your own in the dark is all very well for people like the Nicker,' he said to himself. 'But I'm more used to team work . . . in daylight!'

This was true: all Hans's previous crimes had been hold-ups done in ordinary banking hours.

When he got to it he was glad to see that the guardhouse door was already open and no one seemed to be around. 'I'll check this out first, then I'll go and shut the gate,' he thought. 'I might get the chance to have a bit of a snooze.'

Inside the guardhouse it was pitch black and Hans couldn't find the light switch. He lit a match from a box in his pocket in an attempt to check the room over. There was certainly a table in the middle of it. 'I'll have a lie down on that,' he thought. 'If I sleep for an hour or so it may begin to get light – then I can see what needs to be done to lock the gate.'

He lay down on the table and went to sleep. Before he did so, however, he had the very strange and rather alarming feeling that he was not entirely alone . . .

Hans Zupp the Hold-up Man wasn't the only person in this story who was asleep at that moment.

Many miles away, tucked up in his kilt and pyjama top, Mr Mackintosh slept soundly beneath his tartan duvet cover. He dreamed of smoke and fire and a flame-breathing dragon in the school kitchen who kept telling him she was leaving and that he'd have to do all the cooking himself. 'Come back! Come back, Mrs Perkins!' he said out loud in his sleep, as he turned over and buried his head under his tartan pillow.

Billy Baxter slept peacefully, dreaming of simple things – like scoring the last-minute goal that brought England the World Cup.

Bob Wagstaff, tucked up in bed in his army house at the camp, was having a very bad night. He had finally managed to get to sleep, but his dreams were filled with scenes where he had to admit to the Brigadier that his car had been stolen. In his dreams the Brigadier became confused with a school teacher from Bob's youth who used to terrify him.

Chief Inspector Bollard, his flat police inspector's hat pulled securely on his police inspector's head and his pyjama sleeves rolled down to meet his black leather gloves, dreamt of arresting Harry Hairy the Hatchet Man again.

In the commando camp itself some of the school secretaries were asleep, but none of them very deeply. They tossed and turned on the hard wooden floor of their barrack room, while Mrs Gunge passed the night patrolling above them, her semi-automatic under one revolting arm, and a horrible look of satisfaction on her face. 'Just wait till 'Arry finds out that I've captured the lot of 'em single 'anded!' she muttered to herself from time to time. 'He'll be so thrilled 'ee might even marry me!'

'If only Mrs Perkins was here . . .' mumbled Mrs Myrtle Dickinson as she turned, only half-way asleep, on the floorboards below her bed.

Actually, Mrs Perkins was not all that far away. Once the Corporal and his men had been hoisted from their trench like fish in a trawler's net, she'd waited for them to be towed out of sight by their captors before deciding that it was time to go into action.

'Right!' she said to herself, a look of grim determination on her face. 'No more messing about for me. There's work to be done, and when a school sec. gets to work she really gets to work! Look out world, here I come!'

She crawled from her hiding place in the bushes, stood up and dusted herself down. 'There are two things a good modern soldier needs,' she said to herself, 'communications and ammunition. I've got the communications thanks to this portable telephone, so ammo is all I need.'

She jumped down into the trench which she had seen so recently being vacated. She took care to bend her legs when she landed to protect her ankles from strain. Then she helped herself to blank grenades, firecrackers and rocket flares from the boxes she'd seen being put down there earlier that night by Corporal Hodgkins and his men.

'I'm not sure if I'm up against the army, or villains, or what, but whoever the enemy is, they won't know what's hit them!'

Chapter Eighteen

*Mrs Perkins decides to
create a diversion*

*

'The obvious thing to do now,' said Janet
Perkins to herself, as she stuffed an extra
couple of blank cluster bombs down the front
of her army tunic, 'is to follow that car and
its net full of soldiers.'

It wasn't very difficult to see where it had
gone. The tyre tracks from the car and the
wide groove carved in the wet and muddy
grass by the rope netting were easy to make
out, even in the darkness.

Janet followed the trail as it snaked between the trees along the side of the large
and impressive commando assault course.
She noticed, in passing, the tall poles that
had provided the two kidnappers with their
gladiatorial fishing net.

She hadn't gone very far when she thought
she saw the glint of moonlight on a shiny
rear bumper and heard the muffled expletives
of distressed soldiers.

She slowed her pace, and crouched low –
like a carnivore approaching its prey. As she

got nearer it wasn't difficult to see what the two villains were doing.

By the light of the car's sidelights they were hoisting the bag containing Corporal Hodgkins and his men into the air!

They'd slung a rope over a high wooden beam that normally formed part of a Tarzan-style swing on the large assault course. Commandos in training obviously used it to get across from one high cat-walk to another and to avoid falling in the shallow pit, full of muddy water, that lay beneath it. The two villains had tied their bag of captives to the free end of the rope and had already got them a couple of metres off the ground.

The soldiers were twisting and struggling like rats in a sack. Several of their arms, legs and heads had slipped through the net's holes and were sticking out.

The net hung there, swaying gently, a writh-ing knot of military humanity.

'Time for a diversion . . .' thought Janet Perkins to herself. She was just moving to a new vantage point behind some logs to her left, when her army boot caught in a trip-wire.

There was a FLASH, and a deafening BANG, and a mushroom of white smoke drifted like a huge ghost into the trees.

'What the heck??!!' said the Nicker.

'Get down! It's the enemy!!' shouted Cracker.

The soldiers in the net squealed and swore, and twisted and writhed even more.

Janet lay flat in the wet grass behind a tree stump; the noise of the explosion made her ears ring.

'Clumsy old me,' she said to herself. 'That's not the sort of diversion I was meaning.' But it gave her an idea. If she could deceive the crooks into thinking that enemy troops had arrived, it might stop them in their tracks, and might give her a chance to rescue the soldiers!

She pulled from her pockets and tunic jacket the ammunition she'd collected in the trench. 'SMOKE GRENADE' said the first label she could make out. 'A bit more smoke would certainly help to confuse them,' she said, and pulling out the pin, she lobbed the grenade into some bushes on her right.

Once the smoke was flowing nicely from the bushes, and the men in front of her – both captors and captives – were coughing and spluttering, she unleashed a couple of rocket flares. Then, using the cover of the smoke screen she ran round behind it to take up a new position, from which she chucked a blank cluster bomb into the water-filled trench beneath the swing.

The resulting explosion and small tidal wave sent a column of muddy water into the air like a naval depth charge. It hit the bag of soldiers, and returned to earth to soak Cracker Crawford and the Nicker.

'We're surrounded!' yelled the Nicker with panic in his voice.

'Keep calm, you idiot!' replied Cracker excitedly.

With the skill of an expert ten-pin bowler Janet lobbed a series of blank grenades and firecrackers that set the woods ringing with explosions.

'Let's get to the car!' whispered Cracker to the Nicker hoarsely, as a rocket struck a tree to his left and exploded in a shower of sparkling light.

They set out towards the car on hands and knees, though with all the smoke it was difficult to be certain where it was.

Janet was now running round the scene of the battle, pausing behind a tree from time to time to let off another piece of ammunition. 'I'll move in soon,' she thought, 'but not till I'm good and ready.'

She was just crossing an open space between a large bush and a fallen tree when Cracker, who had found the car and had got into the driving seat, switched on the powerful headlamps.

The twin beams of light shone straight on to the startled figure of Mrs Perkins, silhouetting her against the swirling grey smoke.

'It's a soldier!' yelled Cracker. 'Let's get him!'

The Nicker leapt into the passenger seat and slammed the car door shut. 'He's done for!' he shouted as he did so.

The car engine roared into life and, with back wheels spinning over the damp ground, it shot like a charging bull straight at Mrs Perkins!

She did what you, or I, or Kevin Costner would have done. She turned on her heels and ran as fast as her army boots could carry her.

As she sped through the grounds she noticed that to the east the sky was already streaked with strips of early-morning light.

Not far off someone else was noticing the signs of approaching day. Hans Zupp, still lying on the table in the guardhouse, down by the camp's main entrance, had just opened one eye and had realized that there was slightly more light in the guardhouse than when he had entered it for a sleep a few hours earlier.

What he also noticed – and it totally terrified him – was that indeed he was *not* alone.

The ghost of a soldier dressed only in underpants was getting out from under the table!

He hardly had time to scream before Private Peacock, coming to his senses for the first time since his near-fatal blow from Mrs Gunge the day before, picked up a wooden chair and smashed Hans over the head with it.

Chapter Nineteen

The start of another day . . .

*

Mr Mackintosh had also seen the streaks of dawn in the eastern sky. They'd woken him up, so he'd got dressed, eaten a couple of saucepanfuls of porridge, and gone off to school.

By the time he'd got there, and parked his car, children from Miss Patel's class were arriving from every direction. He noticed that they looked happier than usual – no doubt because they knew they were going to have a day out of school.

Most of them arrived in good time, and were soon lined up outside the garage, near the school dustbins, that housed the elderly school bus that was to take them to the camp.

Mr Mackintosh unlocked the garage and backed the bus out so that the children could climb aboard. Then he checked on Miss Patel's register that everyone was there: only one child was missing – Belinda Bollard.

Mr Mackintosh was just going to ask if anyone knew where Belinda might be when, with a squeal of brakes, a police car drew up beside the bus. While Belinda got out of the passenger side, Chief Inspector Bollard wound down his window: 'Good morning, Mr Mackintosh. Sorry we cut it a bit fine, Belinda couldn't find her school bag.'

'Och, that's all right, Chief Inspector, we're not quite off yet. Still, I'm glad she's made it, we're all going to do a bit of riot control and guerrilla warfare with the army. They're retraining my school secretary.'

'Yes,' replied the Chief Inspector. 'Belinda was telling me all about it. It sounds very interesting – just my line of country really. I might look in at the camp later this morning to see how you're all getting on. I might learn something!'

'Good,' said the Head Teacher cheerfully. And, having counted the children one last time, they all climbed aboard the bus and chugged off up the road.

When they arrived at the main entrance of the military camp, Mr Mackintosh was more than a little surprised that the only person in the guardhouse by the gate appeared to be a rather confused soldier, dressed only in his underpants and with a large bump on his forehead.

'In you go, mate,' said Private Peacock, going cross-eyed and trying to salute. His

head hurt terribly, and he wasn't really quite sure where he was. He'd started the day by apprehending an intruder in his guardhouse and clocking him with a chair, but the exertion of tying him up to the leg of the table had left him exhausted and confused. Once the coach had disappeared up the drive, Peacock sank on to the guardhouse floor and went back to sleep.

The grey streaks of approaching day that had been spotted by Mrs Perkins as she fled from the vicinity of the Tarzan swing, and that had also helped to wake Hans Zupp, Private Peacock, and Mr Mackintosh, had also been

seen by Hairy Harry the Hatchet Man.

He'd spent rather a frustrating night in the Brigadier's tank. He'd motored round and round the military camp, but the tank was very slow, and because he'd only got a small slit to look out of, navigation had been very difficult. There didn't seem to be a school secretary in sight, nor for that matter any soldiers. It was all rather puzzling, and now that daylight had come he had to admit that he wasn't really quite sure where he was.

He stopped the tank and climbed up the ladder that led to the top of the turret. He opened the hatch. It was good to smell the fresh morning air, for the inside of a tank is very stuffy and smells of diesel oil.

'Per'aps if I take a look round I may be able to get me bearings,' he said out loud.

Sure enough, on a nearby tree he spotted a small sign post that pointed right and said 'Parade Ground'.

'That's where I've got to get to!' said Harry, pleased with himself, and he climbed back down into the driver's seat.

As he did so he passed the door of the ammunition locker that contained Brigadier Bletherington-Gore. Harry opened it and looked inside. The Brigadier was lying down inside the locker, rather like a large torpedo. He looked very cramped, and very cross!

''Allo, Brigadier, matie! 'Ow you getting on?' joked Harry with a hideous hairy grin.

'You'll suffer for this, MY MAN!' roared the Brigadier, his face even more like a Dayglo beetroot than before. But Harry just laughed and resumed his place in the tank's driving seat.

He revved the engine, released the brake and prepared to turn to the right.

I can't tell you yet what happened next . . .

Chapter Twenty

*In which we discover similarities
between Mrs Perkins and a fox*

*

Have you ever wondered what a fox feels like,
pursued mile after mile across open country-
side by a pack of hounds who are just longing
to tear it into little pieces?

Well that's what Mrs Perkins felt like when
she turned on her heels and fled from the
Nicker and Cracker Crawford.

And, just like a fox, she knew that the best
thing to do would be to find some cover – a
clump of trees, for instance, where the car
couldn't go. But try as she might she couldn't
see one, and she didn't exactly have the
luxury of being able to stop and look around.
The roaring car was never very far from her
heels, and she was much too busy running-as-
she-had-never-run-before to look at the view!

At one time she did manage to duck down
into some gorse bushes, and by wriggling
from one to another on her stomach she
thought she might have thrown off her
hunters.

They had had to stop the car and, taking

walking sticks from the boot, they had gone from bush to bush, shouting and banging the sticks into them, hoping to flush her out.

Mrs Perkins lay there, breathless, beads of perspiration bespangling her brow. At one time the hunters seemed to be moving well away from her, and she even considered whether it might be possible to get to their car before they did, and drive off. Unfortunately they began to retrace their steps almost instantly and the chance of escape passed.

In fact things became a lot worse. They were definitely coming in her direction. She was almost inside a very large gorse bush, but she knew that she was by no means invisible, especially since it was now daylight.

By the time that Cracker and the Nicker were looking in the very next bush to hers, she knew that she'd have to make another run for it.

She sprung to her rather tired feet and, crouching as low as she could, she sped off like a startled hare.

'There he goes!' yelled the Nicker.

'Get the blighter!' added Cracker Crawford.

The crooks then made what may well have been a small tactical error. If they had set off on foot after poor Mrs Perkins, they would probably have caught up with her quite quickly. She'd already covered a good distance and was probably near the edge of her operational limits. (No school secretary alive can run flat out for more than five or six miles.) But the Nicker shouted: 'Quick, Cracker, into the car!' and so they lost several seconds getting back to their vehicle.

Janet darted down a small muddy track, and coming to a small row of army houses she leapt as best she could over a garden fence, along beside some dustbins, and down a front path before emerging on to a small roadway.

The car did its best to follow. It ploughed through a hedge, crossed the front lawn belonging to one of the houses, brought down a washing-line, and plunged off up the road in hot pursuit.

It just happened that the hedge, lawn and washing-line that it ruined in the process belonged to none other than Bob Wagstaff, the Brigadier's driver.

He had just woken from his terrible dreams, had put on his uniform, and was just leaving his front door in order to walk to the Brigadier's house and admit to him that he'd lost his commanding officer's car.

He was more than a little surprised therefore when the car in question suddenly roared through his front hedge, ripped across his lawn, and disappeared up the lane that led to the centre of the camp!

Bob Wagstaff blinked a couple of times, rubbed his eyes, then leapt on to his eight-year-old's mountain bike and set off up the road, pedalling furiously.

The car, meanwhile, had nearly caught up with Janet though she had managed to gain some distance from it by running twice round a small roundabout at an intersection of two tracks. Cracker nearly turned the car over in his efforts to corner that tightly at speed!

But, like a fox near the end of a day's hunting, Janet was very nearly done for. Her legs ached terribly, her heart thumped within her army tunic, and her head throbbed painfully.

She was on her very last legs when she saw something that, exhausted though she was, greatly surprised and even encouraged her . . .

The St Gertrude's school bus was coming up the drive to her left. She could even see Mr Mackintosh in the driving seat.

With super-human effort she dashed across the grass towards it, the staff car's tyres screeching behind her.

'Help! HELP!!!' she yelled. 'THEY'RE TRYING TO KILL ME!!' Mr Mackintosh, still puzzled by the weird sentry dressed only

in underpants, was even more surprised to recognize his own school secretary, in army uniform, obviously fleeing for her life from a large car draped in washing.

'We're coming!' he yelled back to her, and pressing the accelerator to the bus's ancient floorboards he swung to the left and started crossing the grass towards her.

Then things happened very quickly.

Janet felt the front bumper of the car touch the back of her leg. In near-panic she started to zig-zag, like a rugger player on his way to a spectacular try, then, spotting some tall trees to her right she did a final side-step and shot round a blind corner beside them, rolling into the undergrowth as she did so.

The car, driven by Cracker Crawford, shot round the blind corner too, followed by the school bus, driven by Mr Mackintosh.

I can now tell you something that neither of these drivers knew at the time, though they were soon to discover it.

Round the corner was Hairy Harry, in his tank, just releasing the handbrake, and easing the mighty machine forward on its intended journey to the parade ground.

Chapter Twenty-One

*In which one or two people suddenly
have to decide what to do next*

*

KER-RRRRUUUUNCHCHCHCH!!!!!!!

The Brigadier's car hit the Brigadier's tank
head-on, and a split second later the school
bus hit the back of the car.

It was like two particularly large and angry
rhinos running full tilt, one after the other
into the front of an especially solid brick
wall!

The noise of the crash split the air, and
sent rooks in distant rookeries cackling and
wheeling into the early morning sky.

Even the captive school secretaries, not far
off in their dormitory, heard it, and – because
of the nervous state they were in – many of
them thought it was probably the end of the
world.

The front of the tank crumpled, but it still
looked quite like a tank. The car was another
matter! Smoke, steam and licks of flame
sprung from its tangled remains, the bonnet
ended up in the boot, the doors flew off, and
flying glass went everywhere.

The Nicker didn't exactly fly everywhere, but he did fly through the windscreen. He also flew over the top of the crumpled tank, before landing some distance beyond it in a hydrangea bush.

Mr Mackintosh had been going as fast as the bus could manage, and was nicely in line with the back of the car when it had swung round the corner and into the tank. He had done well to get the brakes on at all, but it was too late.

The impact was terrific. Mr Mackintosh's world went blank.

Luckily the bus had spun slightly to the left when it hit the back of the car, and the passenger doors were not badly damaged. The children, bruised, bothered and bewildered, climbed out on to the reassuring firmness of the grass.

In the oily depths of the mighty tank something stirred. It was Hairy Harry. He ran his hairy-palmed hand over his hairy forehead to be sure that it was still there, and checked himself over for punctures. To his relief and surprise there was no blood anywhere, and he slowly came to the conclusion that he was OK.

Because the impact of the speeding car crashing into the tank had shut the flap that he had been looking through, Harry had very little idea what had happened. He thought he might have been blown up by a bomb, but there was no way of checking because he couldn't see out. He set off up the small ladder to the hatch in the tank's turret to take a look . . .

As you know, Mrs Perkins had avoided the impact of the crash by rolling into the undergrowth. She heard the bang, looked up and saw the awful carnage, and lay for a second or two, exhausted, wondering what to do next.

But she didn't wait very long (the average fox would have needed much longer to recover). The moment that she saw the children coming out of the crashed bus she responded to the instinct all school secretaries have to help children in distress. The villains and their car were obviously no longer a danger to her, so she stood up, pulled some grass and bits of twig from her hair, and prepared to assist the crash victims.

Luckily for her, Hairy Harry the Hatchet Man didn't spot her when he opened the lid of the tank.

Hairy Harry is a pretty unpleasant piece of work even when he's in a goodish mood. When he's angry he's lethal!

And he was angry now. The school secretary kidnap scheme seemed to have gone hopelessly wrong. There was no sign of any of his gang nor of any potential ransom victims. He'd spent the entire night trundling round in a tank, going nowhere fast, and now he'd obviously been nobbled by an army car and bus.

Harry, like any rat or snake, is particularly dangerous when he's cornered – he was cornered now.

In a blind rage he lost the power of reason – never all that strong in his case anyway – and decided that the only constructive thing he could do was to capture a hostage, make a run for it, and negotiate a ransom and his own escape from the whole ghastly fiasco later.

He looked round for a suitable victim.

All he could see, as the clouds of smoke and steam wafted from the mangled wreckage of the three vehicles, were a lot of kids. Harry knew from experience that kids are rotten as hostages: no one pays the ransom. They're worthless.

But then his eyes spotted the slumped form of Mr Mackintosh in the driving seat of the bus. 'Arrr!' thought Harry to himself. 'A teacher, and a wounded one at that. Could be just what I'm looking for!'

He leapt off the tank like a gorilla swinging down from a tree. In a couple of lumbering strides he was at the side of the bus. He

ripped away the driver's door, which was still attached to the bus by only one hinge, and dragged poor Mr Mackintosh from the seat. Then he tucked him under his hairy great arm and ran off towards the woods with him!

Mrs Perkins saw him do it. She went into action straight away, as you'd expect. 'Come on, Class 4B, he's capturing Mr Mackintosh. After him! But be careful!'

And Mrs Janet Perkins and the children set off across the grass in pursuit of the disappearing figure of Hairy Harry.

I haven't told you yet what happened to Cracker Crawford. Although the car he had been driving was very crumpled, it was also large and quite strong. So, although Cracker had hit his head on the roof and the steering wheel had thumped him painfully in the chest, he was still alive.

He'd probably been unconscious for a minute or two, but when he came round he found that he was sitting in the middle of a mess of tangled steel.

He pulled himself to his feet, swaying slightly, and decided to get going while the going was good.

No one was in sight, so he limped off in the opposite direction to the one Harry had taken, and slipped out of sight behind some long low army huts to lick his wounds.

The Nicker on the other hand was comparatively well and happy! The hydrangea bush he was sitting in was a very large and soft one, and after his flight over the top of the tank it had cushioned his landing excellently.

He stood up and brushed himself down before preparing to steal away.

What stopped him stealing away was a soldier who arrived at the scene of the accident on a child's mountain bike.

Bob Wagstaff saw the Nicker standing up in the bush: he also saw the ruins of his precious car!

He recognized the Nicker from his meeting with him in the pub the morning before.

'Oi!' he said to the Nicker, while getting off the bike: 'YOU'RE THE BLOKE WHAT NICKED MY CAR YESTERDAY!'

Before the Nicker had the chance to get out of the bush, or do anything else, Driver Bob Wagstaff walked up to him.

'I've got something for you,' he said.

'Oh? What?' asked the Nicker.

'THIS!' said Bob, and he gave him a hefty punch on the nose.

Chapter Twenty-Two

In which Cracker Crawford meets
Mrs Gunge in strange circumstances

*

Hairy Harry had been so occupied with driving the real tank that, as you know, he hadn't even noticed the small joy stick at his right elbow. By mistake he'd nudged it from time to time throughout the night, and the decoy tank, its insides brimming with flares and explosives, had spent a lot of time careering around with no particular sense of direction.

As luck would have it the decoy tank had actually arrived in the middle of the camp well before Harry had, and in the early hours of the morning it had come to rest beside a long low army hut.

Unlike a radio-controlled toy car it didn't have the ability to knock into things, spin off, and start again in the opposite direction. Instead, its caterpillar tracks had jammed against the wall at the end of the building and there it had ground to a sorry halt, its wheels spinning for an hour or two until its battery finally died and its motor fell silent and still.

The hut it had come to rest against wasn't just any old hut. It was the dormitory building that contained Mrs Gunge and her captive school secretaries!

Cracker Crawford, still a bit confused but delighted to have got away from his recent accident without fatal injury or being spotted by any stray soldiers, staggered round the end of a building and immediately saw the tank resting against the end wall of another one.

'Hey!' he said out loud. 'A tank! Maybe I could use that to get away!'

The thought that the tank might have dud, or better still live ammunition, sent a thrill through his battered frame.

Weak as he was, he somehow managed to get up on to the back of the tank, and reach the top of the turret. He was just looking for its hatch when he trod on one of the tank's several detonator pads.

The noise of the recent car accident had been considerable, but was nothing compared to the sound made by the decoy tank.

BBBBBAAANNNNGGGGG G G G!!!!!!!!!!!

A sheet of light hit the sky. Flares flew in all directions. It was as if a spark had got into the largest box of fireworks you can imagine!

The tank was designed to disintegrate, and that's what it did.

Two other things happened as well. The first was that the explosion blew out the end wall of the dormitory hut, and second was that Cracker Crawford shot off into the sky like an unguided missile!

The minute the wall blew out, the dormitory filled with smoke, and water started gushing from pipes where basins and a lavatory had been ripped apart by the blast. These were excellent escape conditions for the school secretaries. Not bothering to check where Gunge was, or if she had her gun trained on them, they shot out through the hole in the wall with the speed of rabbits who want to get away from a Rottweiler.

Coughing and spluttering, they spilled out into the fresh air and hurled themselves down on the dewy grass behind any cover they could find.

Luckily for them Mrs Gunge had been at the far end of the hut, so she hadn't been able to impede their flight.

However, once she'd picked up the semi-automatic from beside the chair where she'd been sitting on guard, Gunge went into action.

She too came out through the hole in the wall, this time a bit more like a Rottweiler than a rabbit. Her index finger was curled in readiness round the gun's trigger.

'I'LL SHOOT THE LOT OF YER!!' she yelled angrily, like Rambo, in a swirl of smoke.

The only thing that stopped her opening fire was that Cracker Crawford had now finished flying into the sky and was rapidly coming down again.

He came down slap-bang splat on top of her.

Chapter Twenty-Three

*'Honestly, the things a
school sec. has to do!'*

*

'There he goes, Mrs Perkins!' said Billy
Baxter.

He was running beside her, at the head of
a large group of children. 'He's heading for
the trees!'

Billy was right. Hairy Harry was striding
away from them with Mr Mackintosh tightly
held under one arm. He looked more like an
orang-utang than ever.

Moments later Harry had plunged into a
dense thicket, and the only sign that he was
in there was the sound of breaking branches
as he smashed his way through the undergrowth.

'Right, Billy,' said Mrs Perkins, panting.
'Stay near me but try really hard to see where
he goes, and tell all the children to be careful.
He's very dangerous.'

Then, leading the children like some lone
huntsman at the head of a pack of hounds,
she too plunged into the woods.

Harry was showing no signs of slowing

down, even though Mr Mackintosh must have been very heavy. He ran along several narrow woodland paths, crossed deep ditches and hurdled many bushes of various heights.

Then Harry saw something that brought a small smile to his horrible face. There, in front of him, was the start of the army commando assault course! 'This is where I'll throw them off! They'll never catch me now!' he said to no one in particular.

He chucked Mr Mackintosh over his shoulder. The Head Teacher gave a small groan as he did so. Then Harry ducked down and managed to run, still at high speed, through a large sewer pipe that formed the first of the assault course obstacles. Then he scrambled up a high wall. He crossed an area covered with car tyres and ran under some poles that should have had a climbing net hanging from them. Then he started heading up a narrow plank that formed a catwalk high up into the trees.

When Mrs Perkins, Billy Baxter, Wes Richards, Brian Fottleton, Sharon White, Belinda Bollard and the other children arrived at the sewer pipe they were just in time to see Harry disappearing into the tree tops. He looked like some wild man of the the forest, especially with Mr Mackintosh draped over his rounded shoulder.

'Right, Billy!' said Mrs Perkins, 'I'm going after him. Here's what I want you and the others to do . . .'

She spoke to Billy forcefully, and he nodded from time to time to show that he understood.

Then, while Billy Baxter led the children away down a track to the left of the course, Mrs Janet Perkins rolled up her sleeves and went into action.

She managed the sewer pipe quite easily, though running while bent over made her back ache.

The high wall was more difficult, but after a couple of tries she managed to jump high enough to get a hand on the top of it, and after a lot of straining and struggling she got over it. 'Phew!' she said as she landed on the muddy ground on the other side. 'It's probably a good thing that I haven't had any breakfast!'

She ran quite deftly through the collection of car tyres scattered in her path, stepping in them carefully, though it was more difficult than she thought it would be.

Then she ran up a ramp made of large horizontal poles, and dropped down into a sand-pit.

She ran along a single slippery pole, before arriving at the part of the course that went high into the trees.

She drew a deep breath. 'All right, you brute, I'm coming to get you!' (John Wayne would have been proud of her.) 'Honestly, the things a school sec. has to do!' she added under her breath.

She set out, treewards. The catwalks were very narrow, usually made of single planks or poles. In some places there were small battens forming steps, and in particularly treacherous places there were helpful handrails made from rope.

She came to a rope ladder. It was still swaying from when Hairy Harry had used it. She was panting heavily now, but she continued onwards and upwards. As you know, she's that sort of person.

The rope ladder took a lot out of her, and she paused momentarily on a tiny wooden platform at the top of it. As she did so she spotted Hairy Harry and her Head Teacher. They were about three trees ahead of her. Good, she was catching up with him!

Harry turned and spotted her. 'Give up, mate! Yer wasting your time! If you get any closer I'll chop him into more chunks than a tin of dog food!'

'Stupid oaf,' thought Janet, ignoring him. She came to a rope bridge between two pine trees. It was made up of only three strands of rope. One was for walking on, the other two

were handrails. It swayed and dipped precariously as she trod carefully across it.

'Damn it!' said Harry out loud as he turned and saw her. 'I should have cut that through with me axe! I don't know who that soldier is, but they certainly breed 'em tough here. I thought I'd have thrown him off long ago.' Deep down in Harry's unpleasant interior, a slight fear, or apprehension stirred. 'I'll have to make one big effort to get away from him . . .' he thought to himself.

Harry ran down a plank that sloped away from him, and raced up another that climbed again, steeply. The Head Teacher was getting

pretty heavy, and Harry even contemplated dropping him and carrying on unhindered by the extra weight, but he thought better of it. If you're as horrible as Hairy Harry the Hatchet Man you never know when a hostage – or human shield – might come in handy.

He was thinking about these things, and so not concentrating quite as well as he should have been, when the catwalk he was running along suddenly stopped.

Harry, with Janet Perkins close in pursuit, had arrived at the assault course's last obstacle: the large Tarzan rope swing.

Chapter Twenty-Four

In which things happen fast

*

When Hairy Harry arrived at what should have been a simple swing, where, indeed, his ape-like qualities might have seen him swinging away to freedom, he got a shock.

For a start he wasn't expecting the catwalk to stop so suddenly. He tottered slightly, and slowly began to lose his balance. He didn't simply fall off however, at least not before surveying a scene that caused his heart to miss a beat!

Billy Baxter and the rest of the children from 4B were on the other side of the swing, on the wooden platform Harry should have been about to land on, but they were not alone.

They had with them a net full of angry soldiers! Using a piece of spare rope they had hooked the net back towards them, and were holding it, suspended like a pendulum that's stopped at the far end of its swing!

As instructed earlier by Mrs Perkins, Billy waited for the right moment to give the order to let the bag full of soldiers go.

'NOW!!!' Billy shouted, in the split second when Harry and Mr Mackintosh appeared at the other side of the swing.

As I told you, Hairy Harry was already overbalancing, forwards. The net swung through the air with a mighty swish, and the collected soldiers hit Harry full tilt, head on! It was like a jumbo jet smacking into a hillside!

Several things happened very quickly. You'll have to read fast to keep up with us.

When the net full of soldiers hit Harry full on, it burst. Corporal Hodgkins and his men let out a mighty yell, but while still in midair most of them managed to grab bits of Hairy Harry.

Like an amazing swarm of huge angry bees they held on until they landed in the muddy pool of water below them.

The impact of the soldiers hitting Harry caused him to let go of Mr Mackintosh, so he fell on his own to the ground. Or rather, the water.

As Hairy Harry's body hit the water, six soldiers, led of course by their corporal, strengthened their grip on him.

The children from 4B, led by Billy Baxter, dived in on top of them, and finally Mrs Perkins, arriving at the Tarzan swing just in time to see the splash, jumped in too. Her

army boots landed neatly on the back of Harry's skull.

Then Police Chief Inspector Bollard and a small army of school secretaries arrived. He had drawn up at the camp's main gate about five minutes earlier, and had gone into the guardhouse to see if anyone was about.

His policeman's suspicions had been aroused by the fact that Private Peacock, still wearing only underpants, and looking slightly cross-eyed, had mumbled: 'Thank heavens you've come. There's been a raid! I've caught this one but there may be more.'

Peacock had nodded toward the figure of Hans Zupp, who was tied to the leg of a table.

Inspector Bollard hadn't waited for more evidence. He'd rushed back to his panda car and phoned the police station for reinforcements. Then he'd put on his flashing lights and siren and driven full pelt up the drive.

He'd stopped at the site of the road accident and got out of his car, instinctively reaching for his notebook, but then he'd been approached by several wide-eyed and bewildered school secretaries who pointed to the missing wall of their dormitory block, and the lifeless figures of Cracker Crawford and Mrs Gunge, still with a rifle in her hand, lying on the lawn. 'There's some sort of raid!'

said Mrs Dickinson to him urgently. 'This sort of thing has never happened to me before – not even at Frank Bruno's!'

Then the Chief Inspector caught the sound of the yell that Corporal Hodgkins and his men had let out as they hit Hairy Harry, and he led the school secretaries to the assault course at top speed.

'ALL RIGHT! POLICE!' shouted the Chief Inspector, and he and the secretaries waded into the water. While they fished out several of the children, Chief Inspector Bollard, Janet Perkins and the soldiers got a pair of handcuffs on Hairy Harry's hairy wrists. It took several of them to drag him up and out on to dry land, but there wasn't too much for them to worry about. Harry was out cold, totally done for, and defeated.

One person who definitely wasn't out cold and done for was Mr Mackintosh.

When he fell into the cold water it must have had a refreshing and restorative effect on him, because he instantly came round. It's true however, that as he lay there blinking in the muddy water, he wasn't quite sure where he was, or what had been happening, but then, can you blame him?!

Chapter Twenty-Five

Which is our last

*

When Chief Inspector Bollard's police reinforcements arrived they had several little jobs to do.

They started at the main gate by lending Private Peacock a couple of blankets, and radioing for an ambulance for him.

Then they untied Hans Zupp and popped him into the back of one of their vans, so that he could help them with their inquiries later.

At the scene of the dramatic road accident they began taking measurements and making notes, but it wasn't long before one of them discovered a man lying in a hydrangea bush with a very large, swollen red nose. 'He nicked my car!' said a nearby soldier standing next to a small mountain bike. So they picked the man up out of the bush and popped him in the same van as Hans.

They collected two very dazed individuals from the lawn, removing a semi-automatic rifle from one of them. They went into the van too.

They were then joined by their Chief Inspector. He emerged from a woodland path accompanied by several soldiers, the handcuffed figure of Hairy Harry the Hatchet man and lots of schoolchildren and school secretaries. Mrs Janet Perkins followed, supporting the dazed Mr Mackintosh, her Head Teacher.

Suddenly their attention was caught by a noise coming from the wreck of the Brigadier's tank. It sounded like a door creaking open.

Sure enough, the tank's hatch, on its turret, was opening.

They all rushed over to the mighty but crumpled vehicle.

The red face and rotund body of Brigadier Bletherington-Gore emerged into the midday sunlight.

The door on the ammunition locker that had served as his prison had twisted open in the impact of the tank's recent crash. The Brigadier had lain low for a while, stunned and shocked, but now here he was, as large as life – if not slightly larger.

Following a few quiet words from Chief Inspector Bollard, the Brigadier now stood, shakily, on the tank's gun turret and made the following speech to the assembled audience of soldiers, secretaries, children and police:

'Ladies and gentleman, men, girls and boys,' he began. 'I'm not quite sure what's been going on, but I know a hero when I see one. In all my military experience, I've never come across a soldier as gallant as Mrs Janet Perkins here. She undoubtedly saved our lives. It's been an honour to go into battle with her. She's a credit to her regiment! Three jolly loud cheers for Mrs Janet Perkins!'

The three cheers for Mrs Perkins were so jolly loud that distant rooks rose cackling and wheeling into the sky for the second time that morning.

'I know one thing,' thought Mrs Perkins, as she smiled and acknowledged the applause. 'There must be slightly easier ways for a school secretary to get revitalized!'